OAKLAND TALES
LOST SECRETS OF THE TOWN

Other novels for youth
by Summer Brenner

Ivy, Homeless in San Francisco
Winner of the 2011 Moonbeam
and Literary Classics awards

Richmond Tales, Lost Secrets of the Iron Triangle
Winner of the 2010 Historic Preservation Award
City of Richmond

Proclamation by Richmond Mayor Gayle McLaughlin
for first City-wide Family Book Club

OAKLAND TALES

Lost Secrets of the Town

Summer Brenner

Illustrations by Miguel Perez

Time & Again Press
Oakland, California

CREDITS

"Boogie Woogie Bugle Boy," song written by Don Raye and Hughie Prince and recorded at Decca's Hollywood studios on January 2, 1941 by The Andrews Sisters.

Double-V campaign poster, designed by Wilbert L. Holloway, staff artist at the *Pittsburgh Courier*, Pittsburgh, Pennsylvania.

Idora Park, photograph, Courtesy Oakland Public Library, Oakland History Room.

Dorothea Lange, *Japanese Owned Grocery Store, Oakland*, March 30, 1942. © the Dorothea Lange Collection, the Oakland Museum of California, City of Oakland. Gift of Paul S. Taylor.

Alfred Sully, *Monterey, California Rancho Scene*, circa 1849. Watercolor on paper, 8 x 10.75 in. Oakland Museum of California Kahn Collection.

"We Can Do Anything," song written by Elaine Brown and sung at the Oakland Community School.

"Who am I? What do I love? How shall I live? How can I make a difference?" quoted from *How, Then, Shall We Live?: Four Simple Questions That Reveal the Beauty and Meaning of Our Lives* by Wayne Muller (New York: Bantam Books, 1996).

This narrative may contain offensive words that have been used to reflect the attitudes and parlance of particular historical periods and characters.

An abbreviated appendix of historical references and definitions appears in the back of the book. The full appendix and bibliography are available online at **www.oaklandtales.com**.

Oakland Tales
Lost Secrets of The Town

Cover, map, and line drawings by
Miguel Perez

Book design by
DESIGN ACTION COLLECTIVE

Copyright © 2014

ISBN 978-0-9779741-6-0

Time & Again Press
Community Works
4681 Telegraph Avenue
Oakland, CA 94609
T) 510-486-2340
F) 510-647-8560
www.communityworkswest.org

To the youth of Oakland, California
who may not know
there is a there there

Table of Contents

THE PAST

THE PRESENT AGAIN

ACKNOWLEDGMENTS

For sponsoring the research, writing, printing, and public events, the project is extremely grateful to its funders:

Rogers Family Foundation, Rex Foundation, and San Francisco Foundation

For research and source materials, my special thanks to:

African American Museum and Library at Oakland

Alcatraz Island, San Francisco Bay

Angel Island State Park, San Francisco Bay

Allen Temple Baptist Church, Oakland

Arab Cultural and Community Center

Black Panther Historic Site Tour, West Oakland

Camron-Stanford House, Oakland

Centro Legal de la Raza, Oakland

Chabot Space & Science Center/ Champions of Science, Oakland

City of Oakland Planning Department

City of Oakland Walking Tours

Cohen-Bray House, Oakland

East Bay Municipal Utility District

East Oakland Boxing Association, Oakland

Fairyland, Oakland

Gathering of the Ohlone Peoples, Coyote Hills, East Bay Regional Parks, Fremont, CA

Hall of Pioneers, Oakland Chinatown

Intertribal Friendship House, Oakland

Manzanar National Historic Site, Independence, CA

Mission Dolores, San Francisco

Mission San Jose, Fremont, CA

Mountain View Cemetery, Oakland

Musée Mécanique, Pier 45, San Francisco

Native American Health Center, Oakland

National Park Service

Oakland Army Base

Oakland Aviation Museum

Oakland Cultural Heritage Survey, City of Oakland

Oakland Heritage Alliance

Oakland History Room, Oakland Public Library

Oakland Museum of California

Oakland Unified School District

Pardee Home Museum, Oakland

Peralta Hacienda Historical Park, Oakland

Project WHAT! Community Works West, Oakland

Richmond Museum of History, Richmond, CA

RJOY, Restorative Justice for Oakland Youth, Oakland

Rosie the Riveter/World War II Home Front National Historical Park, Richmond, CA

Rosie the Riveter/World War II Home Front National Historical Park website

Scottish Rite Center, Oakland

Tassafaronga Village, Oakland

The Unity Council, Oakland

Urban Habitat, Oakland

"What I Hear I Keep: Stories from Oakland Griots," Peralta Hacienda Historical Park

Youth Uprising, Oakland

Oakland Tales, Lost Secrets of The Town could not have been written without the many individuals who took time to support the project with their wisdom, inspiration, and goodwill.

I especially want to thank Betty Marvin and Gail Lombardi at the City of Oakland's Cultural Heritage Survey, Educational Consultant Kari Ann Hatch, Awele Makeba, Ann Gallagher, and Carla Riemer from the Oakland Unified School District; Holly Alonso, Leanne Hinton, Ericka Huggins, and Dorothy Lazard for their deep knowledge and attentive reading; and Sarah D. Breed from the Oakland Unified School District for her commitment to the project.

I am exceedingly grateful to Annalee Allen, Raphael Allen, Khawlah Al-Olefi, Jessa Berkner, Hannah Boal, Iain Boal, Isaiah Bolanos, Chris Carlsson, Courtney Cummings, Jack Dison, Chris Dodge, Ellie Erickson, Larry Gallegos, Steve Gilford, Kevin Grant, Moses Graubard, David Hilliard, Jumoke Hodge, Jeannie Johnson, Lewanne Jones, Nathan Kerr, Raymond Kidd, Autumn King, Steve LaVoie, Kathryn Lee, Tamsin Levy, Pamela Magnuson-Peddle, Rita Maran, Richard Martin, Martha Martinez, Vincent Medina, John Monetta, Ruth Morgan, Nancy Nadel, Andrea Nobles, Aree Nok, Jeff Norman, Sue Pon, Amelie Prescott, Wilson Riles, Jr., Brian Rogers, Albert Rojas, Tom Rudderow, Andrea Saveri, Harvey Smith, Karen Smith, Sandy Sohcot, Rebecca Solnit, Betty Reid Soskin, Starr Sutherland, Cosette Thompson, Susana Villarreal, Leti Volpp, Michael Weber, Tra Westbrooks, Jane White, Zoe Willmott, and Charles Wollenberg.

In addition, I want to thank Sally Bean, Phil Bellman, Sarah Calhoun, Maria Carrillo, Renate Coombs, Peter Coyote, Jessica Cunningham,

Lincoln Cushing, Fania Davis, Anthony Del Toro, Gay Ducey, Roxanne Dunbar-Ortiz, Laura Gabriela Duke, Ben Glickstein, Libni Gamez, Lina Hancock, Norman Hooks, Mutima Imani, Eunique James, Michael James, Billy X Jennings, Leah Kalish, Jean Langmuir, Gaye Lenahan, Coco Liboiron, Nina Lindsay, Pearl McCarthy, Jayla Miller, Sara Milne, Juliane Monroe, Jai Jai Noire, Beverly Ortiz, Cindy and Helen Q, Celia Reyes, Christine Saed, Shizue Seigel, Daniel Simons, Amy Sonnie, Maggie Stockel, Janferie Stone, Scott Thiele, Jose Villarreal, Dick Walker, Tassa Westbrooks, Stanley Tookie Williams, and Ron Zeno.

The predecessor of *Oakland Tales, Lost Secrets of The Town* is *Richmond Tales, Lost Secrets of the Iron Triangle*. The concept for the Richmond book was initiated by discussions with Chic Dabby, Rodney Ferguson, Dr. Bruce Harter, Betty Reid Soskin, Marin Trujillo, and my stellar colleagues at West County READS and generously supported by the Creative Work Fund.

Berkeley

Emeryville →

Goat Island

Alameda

San Francisco Bay

▨▨▨▨	OAKLAND BORDER
────	FREEWAY
─ ─ ─	BART
────	STREET
▨▨▨▨	REGIONAL PARK

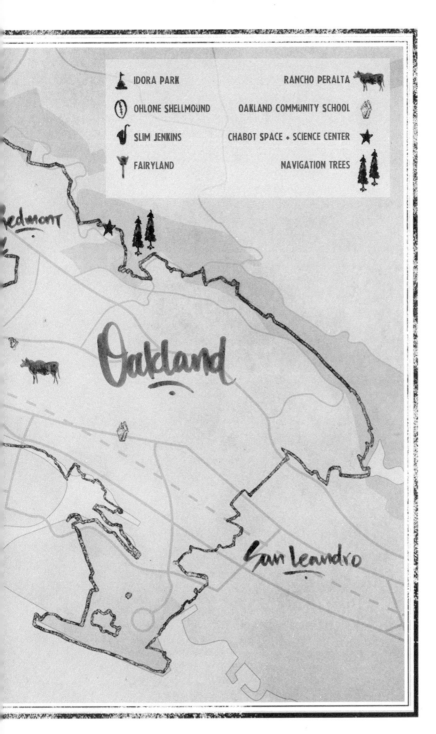

IDORA PARK

RANCHO PERALTA

OHLONE SHELLMOUND

OAKLAND COMMUNITY SCHOOL

SLIM JENKINS

CHABOT SPACE + SCIENCE CENTER

FAIRYLAND

NAVIGATION TREES

Piedmont

Oakland

San Leandro

THE PRESENT

Hold fast to dreams –
For if dreams die
Life is a broken-winged bird
That cannot fly.

Langston Hughes

CHAPTER

FAR WEST
Truth and Untruth

School was finally out. Except for science and
math, Jada Yates had barely passed. It was the same
story last year and the year before. By now, most
teachers didn't expect much from Jada. They understood she was a smart girl who didn't try.

Jada's mother, Sharon Yates, nagged, "If you want
to *be* something, you've got to try harder. You hear
what I'm saying? Every day, I'm out there trying."

Sharon Yates drove a bus for AC Transit, the local
bus company. Driving a bus provided good wages
and good benefits, but it was a hard job. The daily
challenge of maneuvering a big, behemoth machine
through traffic, dealing with unpleasant riders, and
sitting for long hours made Sharon tired and cranky at
the end of the day.

"I want *better* things for you," she told Jada. "I didn't take the chances that came my way. I want you to have lots of chances and lots of choices."

Jada shrugged. Maybe if her daddy had been around, things would have been different. Maybe she would have tried harder, but Jada hadn't seen her daddy since she was a bitty girl. Sometimes she scribbled his name on a scrap of paper. *Randolph Russell Yates. Randolph Russell Yates. Randolph Russell Yates.* She wrote it over and over like a prayer, wishing he'd come back.

"I wish he was here, too," her mother sighed. "Army business keeps that man traveling day and night. I guess he loves the army more than anything."

Although the Oakland Army Base was shut down, older folks in the neighborhood still talked about the good jobs there. Back in third grade, Jada rode her bike from her house on Wood Street over to West Grand and the Army Base. It was a couple of miles, too far for a little girl to go alone. Alone she went, passing factories and warehouses, apartment buildings and an abandoned railroad station. She was scared but also determined.

When she arrived, Jada was uncertain what to do. She looked at the high fences and empty buildings. Then she wheeled her bike inside the empty gate. She hoped to find a guard who would look up her daddy's name in a computer.

She was in luck. Next to one of the warehouses were three men in uniforms.

"Do you know my daddy?" she asked.

"Does your daddy have a name?" One of the men laughed.

"Randolph Russell Yates," she said shyly.

"Never heard of him!" they chimed.

Jada choked back her disappointment.

"Do you know how I can find him?" she asked insistently.

"Not a clue!" they said.

She thanked them and bicycled home, her eyes clouded with tears. That night, she asked her mother, "Where do you think daddy is today?"

"I wish I knew," Sharon sighed heavily. It was hard to be a single mom and make all the decisions.

Jada studied her daddy's photo that she kept by her bed. Although it didn't make total sense, she made herself believe her mother's story. *Why*, she asked herself, *didn't he call or write? Why didn't he visit?* Soldiers got to see their families. Even she knew that!

Auntie Yates was Jada's great-grandmother. Jada loved to visit Auntie Yates in North Richmond. She especially liked to play in the large garden behind the house. One day, she found a baby bird as small as her thumb. The bird had fallen from its nest in the apple tree. Jada carefully picked up the bird and gently laid it in the palm of her hand.

Then she tiptoed into the house. She overheard her mother say, "I can't take Jada with me!"

"She's old enough," Auntie Yates said.

Jada stopped outside the kitchen door. Her mother was upset. Auntie Yates was upset, too.

"You've got to tell her the truth someday," Auntie Yates urged.

What truth? Jada trembled with a deep, unspoken fear as she peeked through the door.

For a few moments, Auntie Yates didn't speak. She stood at the stove, stirring a savory stew made with vegetables from her garden. Carrots, parsnips, onions, and squash simmered in the pot.

"Jada is very bright," she said. "She's going to figure it out on her own. That will be worse than telling her the truth."

"What's she going to think about the truth after my telling her lies?" Sharon cried.

Jada shut her eyes. She held her breath. She was afraid to learn what the truth and untruth might be.

Rat-a-tat-tat-tat-tat, Auntie Yates' knife chopped basil, parsley, and thyme. Jada waited for the chopping to stop.

"We lied because we thought it was best," Sharon said. "If Jada sees her daddy in prison, she'll never trust me again."

"You thought it was best then. Now she's old enough to know the truth. Sharon, please tell her you're sorry. Then tell her where Randy really is."

Jada tiptoed back to the garden. She set the baby bird under the tree. Maybe the bird's mother or father would rescue it. Maybe a cat would eat it. Maybe it would starve to death. Jada told herself it didn't matter. It wasn't her problem.

After that day, Jada stopped asking when her daddy was coming home. She put her daddy's photo in a drawer. She waited for her mother to tell her the truth.

OAKLAND TALES

The House on Wood Street

From her attic room on the third floor of a Victorian house, Jada looked out at the world. She heard the high-pitched squeal of the BART trains, the rumbling traffic on the freeway, the whistles and horns of the trains, and the idling trucks at the port. She smelled the tidewater of San Francisco Bay and the fumes of diesel exhaust. Countering the noises and smells was the beauty of fog streaming over the bridge, the winter rainstorms battering the roof, and the stars glittering on clear nights. Her attic window towered above the streets of drugs and gangs. It was her safe, cozy place. It was Jadaland!

Jada was the fifth generation of Russells and Yates to live in the house on Wood Street. It had been passed down in the family from her great-great-grandfather, Joseph Russell. In the early twentieth century, Mr. Russell worked as a Pullman porter for the railroads when Oakland was the last stop on the transcontinental railroad. Anyone coming to San Francisco got off the train in Oakland and took a ferry across the bay. In those years, there were no airplanes. Cars were rare. For traveling near or far, most people rode the trains.

Many porters bought homes in West Oakland close to the railroad tracks. West Oakland was a good place to settle down. Work as a Pullman porter was an excellent job for a black man. Mr. Russell made only a few cents a day and had to labor long, grueling hours, but it was better than sharecropping on a cotton plantation. It was both far from the nightmare of the Jim Crow South and the crowded slums in the North. Porters catered to white travelers, made beds, carried bags, served food, and shined shoes. In addition, the work garnered respect and generous tips. Before long-distance telephone, the Pullman porters carried the stories, the news, and the political thinking of black folks across the country.

Jada opened one eye, then the other. She yawned and stretched. Sometimes when she lay in bed, she could feel the presence of family who'd lived in the house before her: Joseph Russell and his sons, aunts, uncles, and cousins, and most of all, her daddy.

"Are you awake, Jada Yates?" Sharon called as she hopped up the stairs to the attic. "Have you forgotten that today is the wedding?"

Jada's cousin, Byron Russell from Clawson, was going to marry Lupe Alvarez from Fruitvale. At first, their families didn't want them to marry. Their families were against them.

"Your kids won't know who they are," Byron's parents argued.

"Your kids will be confused," Lupe's parents said.

Finally, the two families came together. They accepted Byron and Lupe's love. They agreed that love made a bridge between them. It wasn't only a bridge between their two families but also their two cultures.

"Everybody is coming from everywhere! New York, Chicago, Atlanta, Sacramento, and Richmond!" Sharon exclaimed, tickling Jada's feet.

"I wish I had something pretty to wear," Jada frowned. Her mother had promised to buy her a new outfit if she brought home good grades. Obviously, that hadn't worked out.

"You've got your purple blouse and striped skirt, your lavender glass necklace and patent leather shoes."

"Moms, they're totally out of style! I hate them!"

"Don't be hating," Sharon reprimanded.

"I have one question," Jada whispered.

"Ask anything," her mother smiled.

"Is Daddy coming?"

The excitement drained from Sharon's face. "Your daddy?" she asked.

"Yes, Randy Yates! Remember him?"

CHAPTER 3

Wedding Dance

Jada met dozens of Russells, Chesters, Harpers, and Yateses. She met the Alvarez, Garcia, and Lopez families, too. Everyone complimented her on her pretty purple blouse and necklace.

"Please consider coming east to college," her cousins from New York and Atlanta said.

"Maybe," Jada said. She knew an eastern college was unrealistic. Nevertheless, it was fun to dream. She hoped she wouldn't end up with a stupid job or pregnant in high school like her cousins Tina and Amira.

The wedding reception was held at the Scottish Rite Center on Lake Merritt. The outside of the five-story building looked like a classic temple with columns and bronze doors. Inside was a magnificent banquet hall with marble floors, ornamental ceilings, glowing chandeliers, tables covered in white linen, and potted palms along the walls.

After dinner, a *mariachi* band from Jalisco played. Dressed in traditional charro suits with tight pants, short bolero jackets, and sombrero hats, they played trumpet, guitar, violin, and *guitarrón* as the wedding party raced to the dance floor.

Following the *mariachis*, a few of Lupe's cousins performed an Aztec dance in honor of the bride and groom. Wearing giant feather headdresses shaped like rays of the sun, silver necklaces with silver pendants, short painted aprons and dresses, leggings made of bells, and feather and fur bands on their arms and wrists, they marched into the ballroom holding shields. An ancient, vanished empire suddenly sprang to life. The dancers looked like Aztec gods. They bent and bowed, swung their arms, and kicked their legs to the beat of rattles and drums. When they finished, the entire room burst into applause.

Immediately, the chords of an organ electrified the room. The crowd turned to see Tony and Sheldon Russell from Deep East glide into the ballroom. Leaping, popping, locking, sliding, splitting, and spinning on their heads and hands, they were fantastic turf dancers who pirouetted on the tips of their shoes and moved

The dancers looked like Aztec gods. The turf dancers moved like jinns.

like jinns in long, sinuous movements.

"I guess that's an Oakland thing," Jada's cousin said in his thick southern drawl. "You know how to turf?"

"I don't turf or surf!" Jada laughed.

"I wished I lived over here," he confessed. "Everybody wants to move to Oakland. It's like a fantasy place."

"Not exactly," Jada said. She wanted to tell him that Oakland was way too real. Guns, gangs, drugs, and fear were real.

The DJ shifted the mood with a string of Motown and swing classics. The dance floor filled up again. Auntie Yates jitterbugged with her great-nephew. Sharon boogalooed with her brother. Jada was glad to see her mother cut loose and groove. "Groove" was the word Sharon used when she danced around the house. Then the DJ put on hip-hop.

"Hey, do you want to dance?" her cousin asked.

Jada looked at him like he was a lunatic. "You must be kidding!"

The first problem was his height. He was a shrimp. Second, he was dressed like a preppie in a navy blazer, a bow tie, and loafers.

"Come on!" he said.

It turned out that he was a really good dancer.

CHAPTER

On Top of the World

As they left the wedding reception, Sharon whispered, "Maisha is staying through the weekend. You hear what I'm saying?"

"I don't like her," Jada pouted.

Sharon cut her off, "You just deal!"

Around Lake Merritt, a necklace of lights twinkled in the water. Overhead the reflection of a crescent moon rippled on the lake.

Auntie Yates hugged her two great-granddaughters, Jada and Maisha. "It's the old moon cradled in the new moon's arms," she told them. "You are my two beautiful new moons!"

Auntie Yates said they carried the whole world in their blood: creamy brown skin from Africa, a flush in their cheeks from Choctaw natives, green streaks in their eyes from Spain and France, and a drop of Chinese. Maybe that described Maisha's cocoa skin and hair. When Jada looked in the mirror, she only saw bad attitude, bad grades, and black, black, black!

Jada told her friends, "My cousin Maisha thinks she's hot. She's not."

However, Jada's biggest problem was Maisha's daddy. Maisha always had her daddy around. That's what divided them the most.

"Come on, girls," Sharon waved. "I've got to get home so I can get up and go to work!"

"Nighty night!" Auntie Yates waved back.

Maisha followed Jada up the stairs to the attic of the old house. "You have the coolest room in the whole world," she said, staring out the dormer window towards the dark bay and night sky.

"You think so?" Jada was happy that Maisha was impressed.

"From our apartment in Richmond, we see a patch of grass. Plus we can hear our neighbors' TVs, babies, and fights! It's a madhouse."

"I thought you liked Richmond," Jada said.

"I love Richmond! But this house is special. I bet Joseph Russell came up to the attic after he got off the train. He stood right here thinking about all the places he'd seen and people he'd met."

"You mean the sheets he changed and toilets he cleaned?" Jada scoffed.

"If I could travel the world, I'd clean toilets," Maisha said. "I want to be a flight attendant so I can fly everywhere."

"What happened to environmental scientist?" Jada asked.

"I guess I want to be lots of things," Maisha said. "Most of all, I want to help make change."

Jada had her doubts. If anything, Richmond was rougher than Oakland.

"We can make a different future," Maisha added.

Jada gave Maisha a puzzled look. Folks said how smart she was, but now she sounded like their cousin Bernard, who was half-crazy from drugs.

From the window, they gazed at the lights on the bridge and listened to the sirens and whistle of a train. The rooftops formed a checkerboard between the tall, majestic shadows of trees: oaks, magnolias, sycamores, and palms. In Richmond, there was only one tree on Maisha's whole block.

"It's a great place to dream," Maisha murmured.

"Like I dream I'm going to be something," Jada said. "Then I pinch myself. 'Wake up, girl, you're dreaming!'"

"You can make it come true," Maisha said confidently.

Jada pointed to the young men hanging out on the corner. "In the fourth, fifth, and sixth grades, those guys had dreams, too. They probably told themselves they'd play ball for Cal or make it to the NBA or be the next rap star. Dreams are like smoke. When a big wind comes, they disappear."

"They had their chance," Maisha said harshly.

"But don't some kids get more chances than us?"

"You're as good as they are," Maisha said.

"If my grades don't come up by the end of eighth grade, I may have blown my chances," Jada sighed.

"You've got to keep the dream alive *inside* you," Maisha said. "Auntie Yates says that's how our people survived."

"I love Auntie Yates, but get real!" Jada said. "Who's paying for your college dream? That's what I mean about chances."

Maisha was quiet. What Jada said rang true. She looked through the window. The young men were still on the corner. Above them, the sky was sprinkled with a few stars.

"I like looking up at the sky," Maisha said.

"Sometimes I look out the window for hours." Jada reached for a chart. "With this, you can track where stars appear at different times of the year."

"You study stars?" Maisha asked.

"When Daddy named me 'Jada Star,' I think he knew I would love stars. If you promise not to tell, I'll show you something."

Maisha twisted her lips with her fingers.

From beneath her bed, Jada lifted a notebook. Inside were drawings of rectangles, trapezoids, triangles, and squares.

"They're constellations," she said. "They're in the sky, but we can't always see them. They rotate with the seasons, and most of the time, the electric lights block them out."

Maisha traced the bear, the scorpion, and the crab with her finger.

"My last horoscope predicted I should be ready for a big surprise in a small package!" Maisha said.

The girls laughed.

"That's astrology," Jada said. "Astronomy is about the planets, stars, and galaxies. The *big* picture, bigger than what's here on Earth."

CHAPTER

Tía Nina

Sunday brunch was the last event of the wedding weekend. Sharon's station wagon was at the mechanics' garage so they took the bus down International Boulevard.

"I've never been to this part of Oakland," Maisha said.

"When you and your daddy go to the Coliseum, you come this way," Sharon said.

"They call it *Deep East*," Jada added.

"It's *deep* all right," Sharon said. "Deep in trouble."

"It wasn't always trouble," Maisha remarked.

"You said you never saw it!" Jada reminded her.

"I meant it was once different. It'll be different again."

"I like Maisha's attitude," Sharon said.

Jada rolled her eyes. Maisha's attitude annoyed her.

Señora Alvarez lived near the Eighty-First Avenue Library. Her house was a stucco bungalow surrounded by flowers and vegetable beds. On the door hung a sign:

WELCOME
FRIENDS &
STRANGERS!

Inside and out, the living and dining rooms, the kitchen, porch, and back patio overflowed with guests.

"Call me Tía Nina," Señora Alvarez said, greeting the two girls.

Jada and Maisha stared at the tall woman with silver braids pinned to the top of her head and the silver earrings dangling from her ears. A large brooch etched with a rose was pinned to the collar of her pink dress. She was lovely.

"Now that Lupe has married Byron, how are we related?" she asked in her melodic voice.

"Byron's mother is my husband's baby sister," Sharon said. She loved to explain family genealogy. "We're also related to Byron's father. He's a cousin on my side. We all went to McClymonds together."

Tía Nina leaned back in her chair. "Does the whole family live in West Oakland?"

"Maisha's family is in Richmond, but her daddy grew up in West Oakland," Sharon said. "We live on Wood Street in the old family house."

"We used to live over there," Tía Nina said. "Before the freeways and BART and post office, Mexicans stayed on your side of town. Portuguese, Italians, Greeks, Jews, Germans, Irish, Swedes, Puerto Ricans, Asians, blacks, we lived together in West Oakland. Everybody got along. Then one day, a tank came like an earthquake and blasted the houses away."

"Everything changes," Maisha muttered.

"Do you *always* have to say that?" Jada muttered back.

"Tía Nina!" A boy bounded through the front door, his jet-black hair flying. He grinned at Jada and Maisha.

"*¡Hola!*" he said with enthusiasm.

"This is my Ernesto! A big boy with big lungs!" Tía Nina said affectionately. "These are Byron's cousins. You must be about the same age."

"*¡Hola!*" he repeated.

"*Por favor*, Ernesto, bring us a plate of *mis enchiladas fabulosos*," Tía Nina requested.

"She always brags about her *enchiladas*," Ernesto teased.

"Because I grow the vegetables and make the *tortillas* myself."

"Like Auntie Yates," Maisha said. "She cooks everything from scratch."

"Tell me, who are Byron's uncles?" Tía Nina beamed.

"Simon is my daddy," Maisha said. "He has dreads and wears a kufi cap."

"*¡Sí! ¡Sí!* Simon and I talked about gardens," Tía Nina said.

"It was my idea to plant vegetables behind our apartment house in Richmond," Maisha said. "It's our Victory garden."

"You're way too cool!" Jada whispered snidely.

Sharon pointed out the twins in the kitchen. "There's Virgil and Jordan."

"Which one is your *papá?*" Tía Nina asked Jada.

Sharon interrupted. "Unfortunately, Jada's daddy is away on army business."

Jada's face crumpled. Another lie in a series of lies. Nothing but lies, silence, and shame.

"He's not away on business!" she burst out. "He's away in jail!"

Jada jumped up and ran through the house to the backyard. Sharon and Maisha jumped up and ran after her. Jada leaned against the fence and covered her face with her hands.

"Moms!" Jada cried. "I've known the truth for years!"

"Let me talk to her a minute," Maisha said. "We'll come right back to the party."

Reluctantly, Sharon stepped into the house.

"Jada, it'll be okay," Maisha soothed, slipping her arms around Jada's shoulders.

"You're always sure about everything!" Jada said. "You can't be sure about this!"

"Daddy says Randy Yates was the smartest man he ever met. He was the genius in the family."

"Was! Was! Was!" Jada sobbed. "It's like he doesn't exist."

"He's still smart," Maisha soothed.

"Not smart enough to stay out of jail! Not smart enough to take care of me!"

"I guess he was only thinking of himself," Maisha admitted.

"Everybody in the world knows what happened to my daddy, but nobody tells me! Nobody thinks I should know! I wish he was dead! At least I could visit his grave!"

Maisha held Jada tightly. "Don't wish that!"

"Why? Then I'd have him nearby."

"He's coming back soon! I know it!"

Jada wiped her eyes. "Are you saying that to make me feel better?"

"I overheard Daddy on the phone. He said he needed to find his brother Randy a job by the end of summer."

Jada gasped. "You heard that?"

CHAPTER 6

Empty Holes

Tía Nina patted Jada's hand. "I'm sorry I upset you."

"It's not you who upset me," Jada said. "I guess life upset me."

Tía Nina rocked sympathetically. "I don't like to upset my young friends, but I see things. Today, I see an empty place inside you."

Jada's eyes widened with surprise.

"My Spanish, African, and Indian foremothers and forefathers, they live in my blood. I carry the sight of my ancestors. Like your foremothers and forefathers, some of my people were slaves in Texas. They ran away. They were lucky to escape the vicious dogs and vicious men who chased them."

"I know about runaways," Jada said. She had read the stories of Harriet Tubman and the Underground

Railroad with its safe houses that led north to Canada. White and black abolitionists hid runaway slaves in attics and cellars. They hid between walls during the day and traveled only at night. They followed the Big Dipper and North Star. Stars guided them to freedom.

"Did they flee north?" Jada asked.

"No, they fled south to *México* where slavery was already against the law. *México* has its own terrible history of *peones* and oppression, but as a new country, it abolished slavery."

"I didn't know slaves went to Mexico," Jada said.

"My young friend, we share much in common." Tía Nina paused thoughtfully. "When we're born, we are open, soft, and full of love. When we see that life is hard, a hard place grows inside our heart. Have you ever had a splinter?" she asked

Jada nodded. She had had lots of splinters.

"A hole inside you is a splinter that no one can see. No one knows about it except you. It gets infected. It turns red. It aches. It makes you angry day and night. Underneath the anger, there's the hurt. That's the empty part. That's your daddy."

Tears glistened in Jada's eyes.

"I see empty holes in the kids around me," Tía Nina said. "Do you see them?"

"Yes," Jada said. She saw them every day.

"Kids get hurt. Kids get mad. Kids get scared. They turn on each other to prove they aren't hurt or mad or scared. They bully. They do bad things with gangs, drugs, and guns. Ernesto did bad things, too. He got in trouble."

Jada could see Tía Nina's African, Indian, and European ancestors shining in her amber-colored face.

"Is his daddy in prison too?" she asked.

"When Ernesto was a little boy, the ICE police broke into his house. They put everybody on the floor. They tore up everything. They dumped out drawers. They cut up mattresses. They found nothing. No drugs, no guns, no stolen money, just a hard-working man and his family. They took away Ernesto's *papá* and sent him to *México*. Little Ernesto, he cried for weeks. Later he got in trouble at school. He was once a good boy, but now he had a hole in his heart. He got in fights. He turned into a bully. He started to hurt other kids."

Across the room, Jada watched Ernesto pile *tamales*, rice, and beans onto a platter. He looked like the happiest young man in the world.

"*La migra* sent his *papá* back to *México*. Later they sent his *mamá*, too. What is he supposed to do? Where

31

is he supposed to go? He has no one standing by him. They placed him in a foster home. He ran away. He turned into a lost boy. He found a gang. He thought the gang would save him."

"Is he your grandson?" Jada asked.

Tía Nina tapped her heart. "He's my sister's grandson."

Ernesto strode across the room. "I saved you the last slice," he said, handing Tía Nina a plate with cake made of *requesón* cheese and sweet condensed milk.

Tía Nina lifted the fork to Jada's mouth. "*Delicioso*," she smiled as Ernesto walked away.

"After Ernesto left the Youth Authority, he came to stay with me. The hardness inside him started to melt. He studied. He read books. He went to the gym. He helped me in the garden. Most important, he began to care about himself."

Tía Nina folded Jada's hands inside her own. A warmth flowed from one hand to the other.

"Look, here's your *mamá*. Why are you making that expression?" Tía Nina pinched Jada's cheek. "All you need is one person standing by you. Your *mamá* stands by you. She protects and loves you. Am I right?"

CHAPTER

Worthless Books

The summer was lonely. Jada's best friends were away. Jada's mother worked overtime. Jada's Auntie Carol had a job, two kids, and classes at Laney. Jada's Auntie Patricia was sick with diabetes. There wasn't much to do and no one to do it with.

However, neighbors helped neighbors. That's how the neighborhood functioned. As Auntie Yates said, "Poor people always helped each other get along with riches richer than rich."

During the summer, Jada was asked to babysit or do small chores. If she was feeling adventurous, she'd ride her bike to Marcus Books in North Oakland. Sometimes she went to De Fremery Pool. She wasn't a good swimmer, but she loved the water. At the pool, she hid by covering herself with an oversized T-shirt. She was confused about the way she looked. Good or bad? Pretty or ugly? Fat or thin? She couldn't tell. Her body changed every day.

On Fridays, Jada usually walked to the library on Adeline. When she walked, she was cautious. She didn't carry a backpack or purse. She stashed her house key and library card in her pocket. She put her books in a grocery bag. She tried to give herself an attitude that broadcast: DON'T MESS WITH JADA STAR YATES!

Most of the time, it worked. Most of the time, no one bothered her.

"Hey, girl! Come talk to us!" two boys hollered across Campbell Street.

"Yeah, girl! We've got something to tell you!"

Although it was a hot day, they had on their hoodies and Raiders caps, fake gold necklaces and expensive shoes. Jada scanned their faces. She saw the holes that Tía Nina saw. Holes for eyes and hearts.

"She ain't talking," one boy said.

"We don't like girls that don't talk," the other boy said. His words slurred.

Jada's heart thumped loudly.

The first boy crossed the street and swatted the grocery bag. "Are you listening? Or choosing to ignore us?" he snarled, kicking the bag.

Jada jumped but held on to the bag. She stared at the ground. She didn't move a muscle. Instead she counted to herself. Numbers soothed her. Unlike people, she could depend on numbers. Numbers were logical and reasonable while people were illogical, unreasonable, and insane.

"Something good is in the bag!" one boy said. "I can smell it!"

"I'm hungry!" the other boy slobbered.

They licked their lips. "We've got us lunch."

"One, three, five, seven," Jada whispered.

"She's finally talking!" The boys howled with laughter.

"Speak up!" they demanded.

Jada stood as still as stone. Her eyes fluttered up, down, and around, hoping a car or pedestrian would appear.

"Maybe she's one of those special ed girls," the boy suggested.

"Yeah, special ed, for sure."

That really made Jada mad. Her cousin Elizabeth was dyslexic. She had trouble reading, but she was as smart as anyone. Elizabeth said it wasn't a learning *disability* but a learning *difference*. She was one of Jada's favorite cousins.

"Knock! Knock!" they yelled.

"Who's there?" one of the boys asked, blowing cigarette smoke in Jada's face.

"Nobody," the other answered. "Nobody's there! Nobody, nobody, nobody!"

"Hey, that's funny!" the boys giggled. Suddenly one of them grabbed Jada's bag and started to run.

"Stop!" Jada called. She sounded weak and helpless. She bit her lip and wiped her forehead. Tears stung her eyes. What could she tell the librarian? They'd probably take away her card. Without books, she was going to die of boredom.

At the end of the block, they stopped running. They strolled along as if nothing had happened. They laughed and smoked and high-fived. They turned around and held up Jada's bag. They opened it and shouted, "Books!"

They dumped them on the sidewalk. They hurled a couple across the street. They stomped on the bag.

The bigger boy raised his fist and started to run towards her. "We're going to get you!" he yelled.

At that moment, a young woman flew through her front door and leapt down the steps.

"Hey, you!" she shouted, clutching a broom in her hand.

The boys froze.

"Does two against one make you feel big?" she asked with scorn. She raised the broom over their heads and slammed it on a fencepost where it cracked in half. "It hurts when it hits your head!"

The boys took off as Jada picked up the books from the sidewalk.

"You saved my life!" she said gratefully.

The young woman grinned. "My name is Asante," she said, shaking her short twists of braided, beaded hair. "I predict you have a long life ahead of you!"

Jada trembled with fright. "I hope so," she said.

"You know them?"

"I never saw them," Jada said.

"You think there's hope for these thugs?"

"Hope?" Jada repeated forlornly. "I guess there's hope for everybody."

Jada *had* to believe in hope. For her daddy's sake, she had to believe.

"I can see that you're a good person," Asante said, lifting the broken broomstick.

"What if they had a gun?" Jada shuddered.

"It was foolish, but when I saw them tormenting you, I couldn't help myself."

Jada wasn't as street smart as her friends Yasmine and Kyra. She wasn't tough. That's why she liked to stay home. Most of the kids she knew stayed home as much as possible. Without an adult, the outside world was too dangerous.

"You have a *right* not to be bullied and pushed around."

"A right?" Jada asked.

"Absolutely! You've got lots of rights. They are written down in the Universal Declaration of Human Rights. Countries sign the declaration, but they don't honor it," Asante sighed. "I get sick of the foolishness, sick to my stomach and sick in my heart. Everywhere, somebody is trying to make somebody else miserable. Sometimes you've got to take a stand and shout, 'ENOUGH IS ENOUGH!'"

"I'm not very brave," Jada said.

"Do you think those boys are brave? Do you think guns are brave? Did you see the holes inside them?"

"I saw them," Jada said softly.

CHAPTER

Mountains and Stars

Over the summer, nobody mentioned Randolph Russell Yates or a date for his release from prison. Sharon didn't bring it up. Uncle Simon and Auntie Yates said nothing. Jada didn't ask. She figured Maisha had misunderstood. However, at the end of August, two important things happened.

First, Maisha invited Jada to go camping.

"Absolutely not," Jada said. She didn't want to sleep on the ground with snakes and bugs and wild animals.

"Come on!" Maisha pleaded. "We'll be in nature!"

"There's nature right here," Jada retorted.

"Please," Maisha begged.

Jada named her favorite local spots. "I've got Middle Harbor Shoreline Park where Moms and I walk. I have the bay, the bridge, the birds, and Lake Merritt."

"Lake Merritt isn't wilderness! Lake Merritt is man-made!"

"Wilderness enough," Jada said. "There are squirrels and ducks and fish."

"You live in an industrial wasteland and call it nature!" Maisha argued.

Jada almost never left West Oakland. Lake Merritt was a special outing. Camping would be a chance to get away.

"How long?" Jada asked, showing a slight interest.

"Four days," Maisha said.

"Do we have to sleep outside?"

"We'll have a tent in case it rains," Maisha said. "Summertime precipitation is rare."

"Maisha, why do you have to talk like that?"

"Like what?"

"Like a showoff!" Jada shouted.

"If I promise not to show off, will you come?"

"Maybe," Jada said.

She wasn't ready to admit it, but her feelings for Maisha had changed. Since Byron and Lupe's wedding, they had grown close again.

"You'll see millions of stars," Maisha said as an extra enticement.

"When Daddy named me 'Jada Star,' I think he knew
I would love stars."

Driving east out of the city, Jada was amazed by the great river deltas, the orchards, and the farms of the Central Valley. They rolled through the dry camel-colored foothills dotted with oaks until they reached the Sierra Nevada. They pitched camp and cooked dinner over a fire pit. As it grew dark, countless stars appeared in the bowl of the sky. Jada was dazzled by the glittering pinpoints. The night sky was the most beautiful thing she had ever seen.

The next day, they hiked up the mountain to a lake. The fresh aromatic air, the mountain meadows, and the clear water were what Maisha called pristine. Maisha was showing off, but Jada didn't mind. She liked the sound of "pristine." It sounded like the world was new.

The other important event of the summer was a call from Jada's science teacher, Mrs. Grant. She called to tell Mrs. Yates that Jada had been recommended for a program at the Chabot Space & Science Center in the Oakland hills.

Sharon thought the teacher had dialed the wrong number. "You mean Jada Yates?"

"Jada Yates," Mrs. Grant confirmed. "Every week, she'll be bused to Chabot with other students from West and East Oakland."

For the last few years, Sharon had worried about Jada. When Jada was young, her teachers talked about her great potential, but since she started middle school, Jada acted as if she didn't care.

"Jada is the most curious and perceptive student I've had in a long time," Mrs. Grant said. "She has never lost her curiosity about the world."

"How much does the Space Center cost?" Sharon Yates asked suspiciously.

"It's free, Mrs. Yates."

"Nothing is free!"

"The program is absolutely free and since Jada wants to be an astronomer . . . ."

Sharon interrupted, "She told you what?"

"Jada knows almost as much about stars as I do. Up at Chabot, she'll have an opportunity to look through the giant telescopes."

"As-tron-o-mer?" Sharon uttered.

"Mrs. Yates, you sound surprised."

"I am surprised," Sharon admitted. "Astronomy is such a grand thing."

"I hope you'll encourage her to stay true to her dreams. I've seen so many bright young people get discouraged and fall apart."

At dinner, Sharon teased Jada, "I guess you're *not* a hopeless case!"

Jada picked at her food. She knew when her mother nagged, it was best to keep quiet.

"I'm saying your teacher called me today!"

"My teacher? What did I do wrong?"

"It seems as if you did something really right, Miss Jada Star! Mrs. Grant chose you to be a Champion of Science!"

"You are joking!" Jada danced around the table. "I've got to call Auntie Yates right now!"

"I guess you're as brilliant as your daddy." Sharon's smile lit up her face. "He is going to be proudest of all."

"You're telling daddy?" Jada asked with surprise.

"I'm not only going to tell him, but I promise you'll get to see him soon."

CHAPTER

POINTS EAST
In the Ring

Ernesto walked along San Leandro Street under the BART tracks past abandoned factories and canneries. He walked towards the gym. His boxing was going well. He was strong, light, and quick on his toes. His coach told him he had good footwork.

"Like a dancer," the coach said.

When Ernesto was boxing, every muscle in his body was alive and on fire. On days he didn't box, he swam at the Sports Center. He loved swimming, too. As a little boy, he and his father had often swum at the beach in Alameda.

If he ran into his old gang, they wanted to know where he'd been. Ernesto's answers were evasive. They tried to tempt him with money. They'd ask him, "You need *dinero?*" They pulled out wads of bills. Ernesto would stare longingly at the cash. He did need money to bring his mother back to Oakland but not *their* money.

He'd try to put them off by saying, "I'm getting by. I've got my job."

"Chopping lettuce?" they mocked him.

Ernesto didn't want to react with anger. He heard his coach's warning: *Leave it in the ring.* That's what the coach said. *If you want to fight, do it where you get a fair chance.*

When Ernesto was in the YA, he read everything he could find. Reading was the only good thing about being locked up.

Back in school, his teacher Mr. Nok loaned him books.

Mr. Nok's family had come to Oakland as refugees from Cambodia. As a boy in Phnom Penh, he'd read many American classics. During the war, their family fled the city. They hid for a year in the forest. For food, they survived on wild roots and mice. When they were hiding, and later in a refugee camp in Thailand, Mr. Nok carried two books in English, *The Call of the Wild* and *To Kill a Mockingbird*.

"They saved my life," he told Ernesto. "No matter if it was the same books, I read them over and over. That's how I escaped the horrors of war."

As Ernesto walked, he thought about his teacher. Mr. Nok told his students. "Reading is your window on the world. Does your house have only one window? Or is it flooded with light?"

By the time Ernesto reached the boxing gym, his mind was clear and calm. He hit the bag. He practiced his stance. He sparred with Leonard Perry, a Native American boy.

"Are you a real Indian?" he asked Leonard. Until they met, Ernesto thought Indians were only in the past.

Leonard jabbed his arm. "Do I feel real?" he laughed.

"I wish I was Indian," Ernesto said. He had read about tepees, hunting buffalo with bows and arrows, and battles with the U.S. Cavalry.

"I don't think so!" Leonard threw a punch. "We are the lowest rung on the ladder so to speak." He laughed grimly. "Most people don't know we still exist, which means sometimes we don't get a rung. The government even makes us prove we're Indian."

"We have to have papers, too," Ernesto said.

Leonard danced around the ring. "But Indians were here before anybody!"

"Like in Oakland a thousand years?"

"We're not local Indians. My people came from far away on the Great Plains."

"That's cool," Ernesto said.

Leonard looked annoyed. "Have you heard of reservations?"

"Not exactly," Ernesto said.

"It's a place where nobody else wants to live," Leonard snorted. "That's where they put Indians. Do we go to reservations like we have a choice? Nah, we go with a gun in our back. After a hundred years of living on the rez, the government decided it didn't like reservations anymore. It decided Indians should mix it up and be *real* Americans. It made up the Indian Relocation Act. They gave a one-way bus ticket to any Indian who wanted to leave the rez. Because Indians were so poor, thousands took a chance and left. That's how my grandma got to East Oakland from South Dakota. She was so scared and lonely, she wanted to take the next bus home, but she didn't have a return ticket. When she tried to find the good job, the good housing, and the nursing courses they'd promised, she discovered it was another lie."

"Sad," Ernesto mused.

"It isn't all bad. We have the Intertribal Friendship House, where Indians from everywhere go. Tribes who never met get together. That's how grandma met gramps. You can come with me anytime."

A friendship house sounded like a place that kept kids off the street.

"There's also the Native American Health Center. That's where I take warrior classes." Leonard grinned. "Peace warrior, that's what I want to be."

"Peace warrior?" Ernesto puzzled.

"Sure, peace starts inside, and then it spreads everywhere."

"So you weren't born on the reservation?" Ernesto asked.

"My mom, Jeannie Gray Dove Perry, was born in Oakland. Her parents changed their last name to Tucci so it sounded Italian. It didn't help. On Thanksgiving, teachers would point to my mom and say, 'She's a *real* Indian.' Afterwards, the other kids called her names."

"That's cold," Ernesto said. He wondered why one group always found a reason to put down another.

"What about your mom?" Leonard asked.

"My *mamá* got ICE'd," Ernesto said.

"Man, that's cold."

Ernesto smashed his fist against the bag.

"My *papá* got ICE'd, too," he said.

"You've got to hang out at my house," Leonard said. "My mom, she's great. She got back her Indian pride. She learned to speak Sioux. She's on the Red Road living in the Native ways, gathering plants to heal, standing up for the land and water, protecting the animals." Leonard rested his glove on Ernesto's shoulder. "You've got to come home with me."

CHAPTER

Hold Up

The next night, they were waiting. Three boys in a Honda Civic and two others in a silver 1995 Buick. Paco Flores was in the front passenger seat of the Honda. José Santiago was in the driver's seat. Diego Reyes was in the back. Hector Lobo was driving the Buick. Ernesto didn't recognize the other boy. No doubt, he was a new recruit.

"Cruz!"

Ernesto wheeled around.

"We've got a job for you," José announced, blowing cigarette smoke through the window.

"Yeah?" Ernesto said, trying to sound tough and indifferent. "I've got a job."

"Washing dishes, man?" José chortled.

"Why do you think they call him *greaser*?" Diego made a joke, but no one laughed.

Ernesto's skin prickled with anger. He glanced at Paco to give him a clue, but Paco's face was blank. *Nada.*

"I've got a job," Ernesto repeated.

"You belong to us," Hector threatened. Hector Lobo had deep scars on his cheeks and a hardness in his eyes.

"I belong to myself," Ernesto said defiantly.

"Yeah?" José spit. "That doesn't sound right to me."

"You live in this hood. You've got the tattoo, *Ride or Die.* You swore an oath," Hector said.

"A fool's oath," Ernesto mumbled under his breath.

"It's about us. We're bonded like glue. We're together like always and ever," José added.

"I took the rap," Ernesto protested. "I went to YA. I paid my exit dues there."

Ernesto wasn't sure about his next move. He heard his boxing coach's voice: *You've got to stay a step ahead. That's your best defense.*

Ernesto felt safer when he was locked up. He was safe like a caged animal is safe. It was terrible. He had made the decision that he'd never risk going back to jail.

"Get in the car!" Hector ordered.

"Paco, tell them," Ernesto said. "I'm not like this anymore."

Paco Flores was Ernesto's oldest friend. They went to school together at Brookfield and Lockwood. It was Paco who recruited Ernesto to the gang. He was small and plump with a long ponytail and a sweet, lopsided smile.

"Better get in the car," he said gently. When he looked at Ernesto, his large brown eyes conveyed the hopelessness of the situation.

"Like a good boy," José coaxed.

Ernesto climbed in the backseat of the Honda. Once, he would have been impressed with the sun-roof and sound system. Speeding cars, loud music, and reckless driving used to thrill Ernesto. He was no longer thrilled. It sickened him now. Riding in a stolen car could put him back in the cage.

"Where are we going?" he asked.

"Shut up!" José said as he floored the accelerator.

The two cars careened down Hegenberger past the Coliseum to the freeway. They continued to fly through Oakland, swerving around 980 to 24 and exiting near Children's Hospital. They headed east to Rockridge and College Avenue where restaurants and cafés lined the street. Outdoor tables crowded with diners spilled onto the sidewalk. Children strolled with their parents and dogs past the bookstores, bakeries, clothing boutiques, and bars.

Ernesto looked at the street, the people, the kids, the dogs. None of them had the mark of his kind of trouble. They lived in another world.

They parked the cars on a quiet residential street.

"YOLO!" José howled.

"Shut up!" Hector said. Hector Lobo was in charge. José shut up.

Diego Reyes handed out ski masks. He handed out guns. He gave Ernesto a gun, a mask, and a paper bag.

"Does everybody know what to do?" Diego asked.

Ernesto started to shake. His eyes blurred. He could no longer remember how he got from the boxing gym to North Oakland. It didn't make sense. It was a weird nightmare where you only think it's real. Instead it's surreal. He pinched himself.

"What is this for?" Ernesto asked, fingering the gun.

"Don't worry," Paco assured him. "You won't have to use the gun."

Famous last words! Ernesto had heard them many times. The words meant nothing. As soon as something unpredictable happened, you panicked. Once you panicked, it was over. You shot, and you got shot. You killed, and you got killed.

That's how Ernesto's friend Freddy died. He died in retaliation for someone else's death. Freddy had nothing to do with the murder, but he got shot anyway. It was a stupid death. Afterwards, Ernesto got Freddy's initials and *R.I.P.* tattooed on his arm. When he passed Freddy's larger-than-life portrait painted on a house on Holly Street, he stopped to stare at the big childlike eyes and the bandana folded across Freddy's forehead. It was a good painting. It looked exactly like Freddy. So what? Freddy should have been alive.

"I've done this a few times," Diego said. "You've just got to stay cool."

"If you do this now, they'll leave you alone," Paco told Ernesto.

Also famous last words! The gang would use him over and over until they all got caught. If the crime was bad enough, he could be tried as an adult. That would mean *real* jail.

"You want a drink?" José laughed and handed over a bottle of rum.

Ernesto and Paco took a swallow. The alcohol tasted like fire. It stung their throats. The effect was immediate. They felt brave.

Brave but stupid, Ernesto thought. The coach's words rang in his ears: *You want to fight, leave it in the ring. If somebody wants to make trouble, you walk away.*

The boys stuffed the ski masks and guns in their pockets. They were jittery as they walked around the corner to College Avenue. Outside a crowded restaurant, they waited for the right moment.

Once inside, Paco's job was to wave his gun and shout, "Nobody is going to get hurt!" He'd practiced a hundred times. Diego's job was to shout, "Wallets, purses, watches, phones! On the table!" Ernesto was supposed to sprint by each table and toss the loot in the bag.

Outside, Hector and José would be waiting, ready to drive to Berkeley. Once they crossed the city limits, they had a better chance of getting away.

Ernesto's heart roared like crazy. His stomach rolled with nerves. The rush used to make him feel alive. Now it made him feel that he was slipping backwards into darkness.

"I'm getting on BART," he said, pointing to the Rockridge station. He handed Paco the mask, the gun, the bag.

"They'll kill you!" Paco cried.

It didn't matter which way the train was going as long as he got away.

YOLO! YOLO! YOLO! raced through Ernesto's mind. "You only live once!" he whispered hoarsely.

"Don't go!" Paco yelled.

Ernesto didn't turn around. He heard the piercing screech of the BART train. He leapt over the turnstile and ran up the steps. He slid into the car and took the corner seat. It didn't matter which way the train was going as long as he got away.

Troubled Dreams

Ernesto's hair and face were wet. His shirt was soaked with sweat. He could barely catch his breath. He was panting.

"Where have you been, *mi querido?*" Tía Nina asked. "Running?"

Ernesto rocked on the balls of his feet. "I've got to stay in shape," he said.

Tía Nina looked him up and down. It was easy to see that something was wrong.

"Making trouble?" she queried.

"No!" Ernesto attempted to smile. "My coach kept us."

Tía Nina looked at the clock. Ernesto followed her gaze. He hadn't realized it was so late. At Rockridge station, he'd jumped on a train that traveled through the tunnel under the bay beyond San Francisco to

Millbrae, then back again to Oakland. He wished he could ride BART forever.

"The gym closed hours ago," Tía Nina said, shaking her head. "Why didn't you answer your phone?"

Ernesto reached in his jacket. "I guess I lost my phone."

"You're a bad liar, *mi querido*," Tía Nina said.

Ernesto couldn't tell Tía Nina the truth. He couldn't disappoint her.

"After the gym, I went to Leonard's house. Mrs. Perry made us Indian fry bread, *jochos*, coconut custard. Whenever I got up to leave, his mom made me stay."

"I can look in your eyes and see the lie. Tell me!" she urged.

Tears sprang into Ernesto's eyes. "I can't!"

She put her arms around him and felt the heaviness inside. *He wants to be a boy*, she thought, *but they won't let him.*

"*Calma*," she murmured.

Ernesto could not be soothed. Who would believe the truth when the world wanted to shut him down? Maybe the world was right. Maybe his fate was sealed. Maybe he only belonged in a gang or jail.

Burying his head in his hands, he said, "I'm in trouble."

"What did you do, *mi querido?*"

"It's what I *didn't* do," he said helplessly.

"What did you do?" she repeated.

"They're an octopus. They wrap around and squeeze until you can't breathe."

Tía Nina was a healer. She cured the body, mind, heart, and soul. *Querer es poder* was Tía Nina's motto. *Where there's a will, there's a way.* She had failed to cure the violence around her. Day after day, year after year, the violence continued.

"They made me come with them," he blurted.

"Who *made* you?" she asked firmly.

"Old friends," he said feeling sick.

"They wanted your company while they looked for trouble?"

A sob caught in Ernesto's throat. His fingertips were still imprinted with the gun and mask.

"Serious trouble," he added.

"Did you go with them?"

"I ran away," he choked.

Tía Nina's chocolate eyes darkened. "Trouble one way, trouble the other. Trouble up, down, around."

"They're coming to find me," Ernesto said desperately.

"Do they know you stay here?" she cried.

"Paco knows."

"Paco is a good boy, but he has no spine. They'll twist him until he tells them."

"True," Ernesto said.

"We'll find a way to keep you safe," she said. "Tomorrow, we'll find a way."

That night, Ernesto dreamed he died. In the dream, he heard shots and felt a pain ricochet in his gut. In the dream, his mother spoke to him: *Te amo, hijo.* His coach spoke to him: *You walk away. That's how a wise man handles trouble.* His teacher, Mr. Nok, spoke to him: *Does your house have only one window? Or is it flooded with light?*

There was a deep and peaceful silence. It was too late for everything.

Searching for Home

During the night, a window in Tía Nina's house was shot. Glass shattered over the carpet. Ernesto jumped out of bed, remembering his awful dream.

"It's a warning!" he said.

"It's not safe for you here," Tía Nina said, folding her hands in her lap.

"It's not safe for you either!"

"They can't frighten me because I've already lived most of my life. Nobody can take *that* away. But you, *mi querido*, they want to . . . . She touched the candle beside her and rubbed her fingers. "I forget the English."

"Snuff," Ernesto said.

"*!Sí, sí!* They want to snuff you out! I won't let them!"

63

Tía Nina lifted a small mirror from the table. She held it in front of them.

"Here we are," she said softly.

Ernesto squinted at the reflection.

"Our blood, it's linked. Your eyes are mirrors of my eyes. Inside them, we are connected through time with people whose names are lost." She held out her hand and touched her ring. "It has four jewels from the four corners of the earth. The turquoise is our Mexican blood as true and blue as the sky that protects us. The African ruby is our blood that was given and lost. The quartz is clear like pure water, the source of all life. The green jade holds the power of love. Protection, giving, clarity, love. You are my thread, Ernesto. That's why I won't let them harm you."

Ernesto smiled weakly. Tía Nina's words were comforting, but her words couldn't stop a bullet.

"Should I go to Mexico?" he asked.

"Is that what you want?"

Ernesto was torn. Mexico would unite him with his family. Mexico would put him out of harm's way. However, his parents left Mexico so he could have opportunities they never had. Returning would betray everything they had sacrificed.

"I want to stay in Oakland," he said. "Oakland is home."

Late in the afternoon, they spoke to his mother, Catalina Cruz.

"Ernesto helps me every day," Tía Nina reported. "He works in the garden. He helps clean the house. He studies. His teachers talk to him about college."

"I'm happy to hear good things," Catalina said. The good things helped to ease the separation.

"There is something not so good," Tía Nina said. "We have to find another place for him to stay."

"*Mi hijo*, did he do something bad?"

"The old gang has started to come around again."

"Is he in trouble?" Catalina was prepared for the worst.

"He wants to stay *out* of trouble. Sometimes that's hardest of all. Sometimes other boys want to take you down with them."

"Without you and me, who can help him now?" Catalina cried. "A thousand miles away, I worry day and night."

"Don't worry," Tía Nina said. "I'll make sure he's safe!"

CHAPTER 13

Randyman

Jada picked up the phone, hoping it was Yasmine or Kyra, home from summer vacation. Most of all, she missed Kyra. Kyra was the funniest girl in West Oakland.

"*¡Hola!*" a melodic voice greeted her. "It's Tía Nina, remember me?"

"Of course!" Jada said.

Jada handed the telephone to her mother. They talked for a long time.

"Ernesto is spending the weekend with us," Sharon announced after they hung up.

"Here?" Jada asked incredulously.

"You have to make him feel welcome."

"Is he in trouble?"

"The world is in trouble," Sharon said. "If I didn't help him, I'd never forgive myself."

"You don't even know him!" Jada objected. She didn't want a strange Mexican boy roaming around her house.

"Some folks want Mexicans and blacks to be enemies. I don't feel that way. Mexicans ride my bus every day. They're like anybody else: some good, some bad, some in between. Their problems are a lot like ours."

"What happened to Ernesto?" Jada pried.

"What if your daddy had left West Oakland when things got bad? You hear what I'm saying? It would have been a whole different life for all of us."

Daddy echoed in the silence around them. It was both a sacred and forbidden topic.

"Randyman had such promise," Sharon said, overwhelmed with regret.

"Randyman?" Jada laughed sadly.

"He was brilliant. Maybe I never told you about his academic scholarship to college."

"You never told me much."

"He was gifted. He was loved. But he stopped seeing his true self. He fell in with dopers, scammers, hustlers, crooks. They were lost so Randyman got lost, too." Sharon wiped her eyes. "I tried to make it right for him. Sometimes you've got to see it for yourself. If you don't see it, nobody can't tell you nothing about it."

Jada recalled the conversation at Auntie Yates's house. She could smell Auntie Yates's stew and hear Auntie Yates's chopping knife and feel the baby bird, the size of her thumb, inside her palm. It was the day she discovered her daddy was in prison.

"I'm sorry your daddy has never been here for you," Sharon said, wrapping her arms around Jada.

"I'm sorry, too," Jada sobbed.

"He's not here, but I know he's so proud of his Jada Star."

Whatnots and Knickknacks

An hour later, Tía Nina's nephew Jorge arrived at the house. She kept watch while Ernesto ran to the car. He lay down on the backseat, and Jorge drove away. Instead of 880, he meandered up the hills beyond Castlemont High and along MacArthur. Jorge used to drive a taxi. He knew every inch of Oakland.

"Have you been to West Oakland?" he asked.

"Never," Ernesto admitted.

"Don't tell anybody you're from Deep East," Jorge advised.

Ernesto climbed out of the car. He grabbed his duffle. Before him stood a three-story Victorian house and a large oak tree. An eerie orange light from the port glowed through the fog. Traffic rumbled, BART whined, foghorns moaned, and a train whistled. He waited for the train to fade into the distance, took a deep breath, and walked up the path to the house.

"Who is it?" Sharon called through the heavy wooden door.

"Ernesto Cruz, Mrs. Yates," he said.

A key turned. A chain clanked. A bolt slid back. A grandfather clock chimed.

"Welcome!" Sharon Yates smiled and ushered Ernesto into the front hall. "Excuse the mess, but I inherited an old house and everything in it. No one ever threw anything away!"

Beyond the hall was the parlor. It looked more like an antique shop than a living room. It was crammed and cluttered with two horsehair sofas, Victorian side chairs, sideboards, whatnots and knickknacks, an upright piano, marble-topped tables, and tall brass lamps with hand-painted shades. The walls were covered with sepia-tint photos and tintypes.

"Are they your family?" he asked, his eyes wandering from face to face.

"The oldest ones are my mother's people after slavery ended. Every freed slave wanted a photo. It wasn't like today. Nothing was instant. They had to wait months for a traveling photographer to get to their house. You can see they dressed up in their Sunday best. A photograph was proof they didn't belong to somebody else." Sharon contemplated. "I wonder if young people now can understand how it feels to be owned."

"I can!" Ernesto insisted. He would never feel free until his old gang let him go.

"¡Hola!" Jada called from the stairs.

"¡Hola!" Ernesto laughed.

"Follow me," she said.

Ernesto picked up his duffle bag and climbed the well-worn steps to the guest room on the second floor.

"Everything is old." Jada coughed apologetically as she pulled aside the dusty drapes, tugged on the window frame, and leaned out into the cool, foggy air. "My cousin, Maisha, calls this house a mausoleum. She's big on big words."

Ernesto stared at the old-fashioned canopy bed, armoire, writing desk, and ladder-back chair. On the walls were more photos and a collection of ladies' bonnets.

"Where's your room?" he asked.

"I took over part of the attic. There's none of this old stuff. Only my stuff! It's Jadaland!"

Ernesto slept on a coil spring mattress with feather pillows and a chenille bedspread. At first, he slept like a baby. Then he had a nightmare. It was the same nightmare that he had had the night before. First he heard the shots. Then he felt the pain. His mother spoke the same words, *Te amo, hijo.* His coach's words echoed, *That's how a wise man handles trouble.* Mr. Nok repeated, *Does your house have only one window?* He awoke in a panic. *Bad dream, bad dream, bad dream,* he told himself.

In the morning, he asked Jada, "So, what do you like to do all day?"

"Not much to do so I usually stay home," she said. "Moms asked me to organize the junk in the attic annex. If you want, you can help."

Stuffed in the unfinished portion of the attic were musty books, old newspapers, cardboard boxes, wooden crates with Chinese characters, and dusty steamer trunks.

Ernesto regarded the piles of family artifacts. His parents had left everything behind in Mexico when they moved to Oakland. His father brought only an heirloom watch and photos of his family. His mother brought an opal ring and a painted portrait of her parents. The *coyote* stole the watch and ring. The portrait of his grandparents was lost when they moved from one apartment to another. Only a few photos remained that he kept in a shoe box.

"Maybe there's a treasure up here," he joked.

"That's the problem! My family thinks it's all treasure!"

They picked through clothes and quilts, linens, crockery, baby shoes, lace handkerchiefs and gloves, large hats with feathers, fans, walking sticks, Pullman porter uniforms, war medals, newspaper clippings, photo albums, and books. Whatever was crumbling or rotten, they put aside to throw away.

Ernesto donned a tweed jacket, a fedora, and a pair of polished oxfords.

"How do I look?" he grinned.

"Like an old gangster!" Jada chuckled. "Those things went out of style fifty years ago."

"What about over here?" he asked, crawling under the rafters. When he crawled out, he was coated with cobwebs. He held a mahogany box in his hand. "What's this?"

"Not a clue," she said.

They tried to open the box, but it was locked. Jada skipped downstairs to the kitchen and returned with a large ring of keys. She picked out the tiniest one and inserted it in the keyhole. It didn't work. She tried a dozen others. Finally, a key turned in the lock. The rusty hinges creaked as she lifted the lid.

Ernesto inspected the interior. "I thought it was a money box," he said with disappointment.

"What are they?" Jada asked, lifting one of the egg-shaped objects from its velvet pocket.

They were all the same size, as large as a turkey egg, with a smooth, hard exterior and a tiny window. Through one window, Jada spied a miniature forest. When she blinked, the forest changed slightly. Ernesto picked up another egg. Inside was the scene of a marsh. Suddenly a flock of birds rose in the air.

"They're bizarre," she said, putting the eggs back inside the box, closing the lid, and locking it.

"They're cool," he said.

"They give me the creeps," she shivered.

"Boo!" he yelled.

Jada jumped. "Okay, you got me! Don't do it again!"

Fandango

A week later, Ernesto heard on TV that two juveniles from East Oakland had been arrested in the Rockridge district for a restaurant robbery. The news said it was the third such robbery in ten days. One juvenile had been shot, trying to flee the scene.

Tía Nina telephoned with the news. "It's no good to come back now."

Ernesto was heartbroken. He'd let Paco down. Maybe if he'd been there, his friend wouldn't have gotten hurt. Maybe he could have stopped them. Now Paco was in the hospital in critical condition and facing serious charges. If Paco died, it would be on him.

Sharon informed Jada, "Ernesto is staying on."

"You've got a Mexican boy living in your house?" her good friend Kyra asked.

Jada attempted to act casual. "He's my long lost brother."

"I guess a lot happened while I was away," Kyra laughed.

"Like in the *big* picture where we're all brothers and sisters," Jada clarified.

Kyra laughed harder. "Have you seen the dude who sleeps on my corner? For real, he is not my brother!"

They laughed together.

"Is Ernesto *fine*?" Kyra giggled.

"It's nothing like *that*!" Jada protested.

On Sunday, Maisha came to supper with her parents and Auntie Yates. Tía Nina and her nephew Jorge came, too. Tía Nina was glad to see her old neighborhood. Much had changed, but many things remained the same.

As soon as the dishes were cleared, Jada and Ernesto ushered Maisha upstairs to the attic. Maisha poked around until she found a trunk with parasols and hats. She tried pulling on a pair of crocheted gloves and high-button boots.

"They fit when I was little," she complained.

"We loved to play dress up," Jada said.

"We hoped to find a treasure," Maisha said.

They stared inside the egg. "It's just a little movie!"

Jada looked at Ernesto. Ernesto looked at Jada. They hadn't discussed if they intended to share their secret.

"What?" Maisha asked eagerly, glancing back and forth at them.

"Ernesto discovered something," Jada said.

Maisha's eyes widened with curiosity as Jada unlocked and lifted the box's heavy lid.

Maisha gasped. "They were here and we never saw them!"

"Do you know what they are?"

There was silence as Jada and Ernesto waited for Maisha to speak. Finally, she said, "You remember Auntie Yates's friend, Misty Horn."

"I remember him," Jada said. She had met him at Auntie Yates's house in North Richmond.

"He's unusual," Maisha said.

"He's scary," Jada added.

"Once you get to know him, he's not scary. Misty Horn knows things other people don't."

"Does he know about these eggs?" Ernesto prompted.

Trembling, Maisha lifted an egg from its velvet pocket. "He has a set like these!"

"They change, don't they?" Ernesto asked.

"Don't play with them. They're dangerous," Maisha said.

"Dangerous?" Jada was skeptical.

"You might find yourself . . . ."

"What?"

"These eggs can do things. They can take you places and show you how things used to be. They aren't toys or playthings. You have to be careful."

"We're really curious," Jada said impatiently.

"If I ask Auntie Yates to bring Misty Horn to supper next Sunday, will you promise to wait?"

Jada and Ernesto agreed, but after Maisha left, they went back to the attic.

"Her warning was serious," he cautioned.

Jada shrugged. "Maisha exaggerates everything!"

"We've seen them change," Ernesto reasoned.

"I love Maisha, but she's one of those know-it-all girls."

"I thought you said they were creepy," Ernesto said.

"If Maisha can deal with them, I can, too."

Jada twisted the key and unlocked the mahogany box. She lifted an egg from its pocket.

"They're dancing!" she cried gleefully, looking through the miniature window.

Inside the tiny window was a dark, handsome man in tight pants, a short jacket, and a burgundy-colored scarf thrown loosely around his neck. His feet made sharp, staccato movements as his arms circled the air. He tapped wildly with his boots and snapped his fingers. Next to him, a woman played the castanets. Other ladies, dressed in rustling silk dresses and silk shawls and holding lace fans, watched with admiration.

"Bravo! Bravo!" they shouted.

Suddenly his arm grabbed Jada around the waist. "¡Fandango!" the dancer whispered in her ear.

He whirled her past the throng of ladies and gentlemen. The shadows of tallow candles flickered, and the aromas of rich food and wine filled the air.

"Help!" Jada wailed.

"What?" Ernesto sounded far away.

"Help! Help!"

In an instant, Jada found herself standing next to Ernesto. They stared inside the egg. The dancer, the ladies, the smell of melting wax had vanished. There was nothing. The egg was empty.

"It's just a little movie!" she said with relief.

Ernesto turned the egg up, down, and around. "But how?"

THE PAST

The past is never dead. It's not even past.

{ William Faulkner }

The Harder We Look

The next Sunday, Misty Horn arrived with Auntie Yates. At supper, Jada and Ernesto scrutinized the peculiar man: his orb of cotton-white hair, his dimples and warts, his penetrating black eyes that flitted around the table, and his animated gestures as he told story after story.

After dessert, Misty Horn asked if he could lie down.

"I'm very tired," he apologized to Sharon.

Jada and Ernesto helped him to the second floor, but as soon as they were in the hallway, he pointed to the attic.

"Are they up there?" he asked, his eyes flashing with excitement as he bounced up the steps. "I must see them now!"

Misty Horn held up an egg. "It's Oakland," he said.

"I don't see Oakland!" Jada declared.

"*Nada*," Ernesto agreed.

"It's the original shoreline at the end of Seventh Street."

"There's *nothing* there!" Jada cried.

"On the contrary, there's *everything* there! Oakland is a kind of paradise. There are plants to make houses, clothes, and boats. There are animal skins for comfort and warmth. There are feathers and shells for decoration, chert and obsidian for arrowheads, bones and hooves for musical instruments, reeds and rushes to weave baskets. Food is so abundant that you only have to gather and cook it. If you look at the edge of the clearing, you'll see a tule hut. Tule is a plant that grows by the water. The Native peoples had many uses for tule."

"We saw pictures of tule in the fourth grade," Jada said.

Misty Horn steadied himself against the wall. His hands shook and his voice faltered. "Pictures are terrific unless you can see the *real* thing!"

"Are you sick?" Jada asked.

Ernesto pushed open the dormer window. "How about a little fresh air?"

"You call *this* fresh?" Misty Horn frowned.

"Sometimes it stinks," Jada admitted.

"In East Oakland, I can smell burning tires," Ernesto said.

"If you have a minute or two, I'll take you where the air and water are absolutely pure."

"Like where?" Jada asked. Even camping with Maisha, they couldn't drink from the lake or mountain streams.

Misty Horn pointed inside the egg. "There!" he exclaimed.

Jada rolled her eyes. Misty Horn was either ill or out of his mind. Maybe Maisha was a little crazy, too.

"Like Lake Merritt?" Ernesto asked.

"Lake Merritt hasn't been built," Misty Horn said, peering into the egg. "What we call Lake Merritt is a marshy slough and an excellent place to find tule!"

"TU-LEE!" Jada and Ernesto laughed.

"It's a short trip, not far at all," Misty Horn coaxed as he closed his eyes and pressed his nose to the window of the egg.

Jada and Ernesto were both familiar with the eccentricities of old people. The best thing was to listen politely and then take Misty Horn back downstairs.

The old man muttered:

The harder we look, the more we see!
The more we stare, the sooner we get there!

"But," Jada interrupted.
"Say it!" he commanded.

The harder we look, the more we see!
The more we stare, the sooner we get there!

"All together!" Misty Horn encouraged.

The harder we look, the more we see!
The more we stare, the sooner we get there!

CHAPTER

The Gift of Time

Ernesto inhaled the fragrant air and the sharp scent of evergreens from trees as tall as skyscrapers.

"Do you see how high they are?" he asked.

"Almost as high as the eye can see," Misty Horn said.

Jada had never seen anything like them, not even on her camping trip with Maisha. Underneath the trees, the air was cool and moist and the sunlight dim.

"Where are we?" she asked warily.

"In the pristine hills of East Oakland," Misty Horn replied.

"East is the beast!" Ernesto high-fived Jada.

"West is the best!" she retorted.

Misty Horn patted the rough bark. "My old friend," he said to the tree trunk. "When European ships came into the bay, they lined up their prows with these trees to bypass Blossom Rock. That's how the trees got their name, Navigation Trees."

Jada was flabbergasted. "How could ships over there see trees in Oakland?"

"They're living giants: hundreds of feet tall, tens of feet around, and as old as two thousand years."

"They're beautiful," Jada sighed with admiration. "I get a crick in my neck looking up at them."

A symphony of wildlife sounds burst from the trees: birds cawed, cooed, chirped, chattered, pecked, and hooted; insects hummed and buzzed; small animals scurried about; and wings flapped. Especially impressive were the gigantic condors whose black silhouettes swept the sky.

Jada was both frightened and thrilled. "Is this where Indians live?" she asked.

"Yes, yes," Misty Horn confirmed. "Their name isn't 'Indian.' In Oakland, they're called 'Huchiun' if they live by the Bay and 'Jalquin' if they live in the eastern hills. We say 'Ohlone.'"

"Ohlone?" Ernesto asked.

"If we follow the path by the creek, we can hike to their village. It's a long walk, but we're in slow time. You won't even notice."

"Slow time, I like that," Ernesto said.

"Slow time is inside you. It existed for eons before the combustion engine and Internet. To feel it, you only have to stop and be still."

They stood with their feet on the ground and their faces lifted to the sun, trying to be still.

"How does it feel?" Misty Horn asked.

"Strange," Jada said. Even if she stopped her body, her mind raced on.

"Slowing down your mind takes practice," Misty Horn said as if reading Jada's thoughts.

"Do Ohlone come up here?" Ernesto asked.

"At certain times of year, the women and girls come to the hills to gather berries, acorns, grasses, seeds, and nuts. Men and boys come to spear salmon and trout in the creeks and hunt deer in the forest. They kill animals to survive, but they never waste any part of what they kill. That's how they live in balance with the earth."

Jada froze as a family of elk strolled nearby.

"You never saw a horse or a cow?" Ernesto teased.

"They aren't horses and cows! They're wild animals!" Jada objected.

Misty Horn intervened. "Nothing is going to hurt you."

When Jada saw that the elk ignored her, she let herself enjoy the ancient trees, the singing birds, the gurgling streams. Adding to the magic was the tinkling of children's laughter.

Beyond the stand of redwoods was an oak grove. Beneath the oak trees sat women and girls in tule skirts. Many had tattoos on their faces and shoulders. Some wore shell necklaces and animal skins. Others carried cradle baskets for the infants. Sitting and squatting, they were busy sorting through acorns that had fallen on the ground.

Jada and Ernesto studied their sturdy brown bodies, their straight black hair, their strong handsome faces, and their tattoos. Mesmerized by the shuffling, sorting, and tossing of acorns into baskets, they fell into slow time.

"They're harvesting food for the village for the entire year," Misty Horn explained. "Acorns and chia seeds are their staples. They gather the ripe acorns in late fall before the rains come. Afterwards, the acorns are dried for months before they are leached and pounded into flour to make *pinole*."

"It hardly looks like work," Jada observed.

"They play while they work. They sing and talk and relax."

Jada and Ernesto didn't understand. Work was work. Play was play.

"Someday, I hope I can work and play at the same time," Jada said.

"If you love what you do, work and play become the same thing," Misty Horn said. "It's about the gift of time."

Reading the World

Jada rubbed her calves. "That's way longer than I ever walked!"

Ernesto mopped his head with a bandana. "I think I'll jump in the creek!"

They waded in the sparkling water. Beside the creek was a willow grove and *temescal*. Misty Horn pointed to the *temescal*'s fire pit and brush roof.

"Ohlone men build fires in the *temescal* to sweat. Sweating is good for body and soul."

Ernesto shuddered. Temescal was near the district in North Oakland where Paco got shot. He sent out a healing message to his friend.

"Where are we now?" Jada asked.

In all directions spread oak trees with gnarled limbs and leafy green branches. Not a street or building was in sight. "I think we're near Oakland Tech."

They sat on the banks of the creek and dried their feet in the sun. "We call this Temescal Creek. It was the largest creek in the area. At certain times of year, it flowed like a river."

"Temescal is a lake, too," Jada said. Her sixth-grade field trip visited Lake Temescal.

"The lake wasn't built until the creek was dammed for Oakland's first water supply. Everyone remembers Anthony Chabot who designed the earthen dam, but we've long forgotten the Chinese who risked their lives to build it. Come along! We've got walking to do!"

In late afternoon, they reached the mouth of Temescal Creek and a village of tule huts. Some were living quarters, others used to store food. Under a *ramada,* women and girls sang and cracked acorns, flinging plump acorn meat into winnowing baskets. Offshore, men paddled tule boats filled with fish, abalone, and duck eggs. On the beach, boys collected mussels, oysters, and clams. Children played *wannuk,* a guessing game, and *trallik,* a game with sticks rolled like dice. Younger kids played with dolls made of oak galls with painted faces and grass hair.

"I guess they don't go to school," Jada said.

"Everything they need to learn is all around them. Morning to night, week to week, year to year, they learn. Men, boys, women, girls, they cooperate and contribute their part. When work is done, they enjoy themselves."

Jada had mixed feelings about what she saw. The skimpy clothes, the feathers and tattoos, the tule houses, the absence of school made her uncomfortable. There weren't any modern conveniences. However, life appeared to be safe and serene, two important things missing from Jada's own life.

"*Mi papá* would love this," Ernesto said. "In Mexico, he is always in the fields or taking care of the chickens and pigs. In Oakland, he never got comfortable. He never fit in."

Jada was thinking of her dad, too. "Hard to get in trouble here," she said.

"Way peaceful," Ernesto sighed.

"Sun, seasons, moon, and stars, these are your calendar and clock."

"Will they talk to us?" Jada asked.

"I'm not sure we're visible. If they do see us, they may think we're not real," Misty Horn said. "Perhaps we'll hear them speak Chochenyo."

"Have you come here before?"

"It's my favorite place and the slowest time of all." A shadow passed over Misty Horn's face. "The Ohlone ways were destroyed. The people were forced into servitude and slavery, forced to abandon their customs and languages, ravaged by smallpox and measles, hunted and murdered."

"Measles?" Ernesto reflected.

"They had no defenses against the Spaniards and their diseases. The Ohlone rebellions were squashed by soldiers from the *presidio*. The Ohlone never recovered from these invasions."

Ernesto listened with a heavy heart. He recalled the words of his friend, Leonard. *Indians are lowest on the ladder,* Leonard had said.

Across the clearing, Jada looked at a group of girls, chatting and laughing. They reminded her of Kyra and Yasmine, chatting and laughing. For an instant, Jada's eyes met the eyes of an Ohlone girl.

"She sees us!" Jada cried.

"Maybe she'll offer us a bite to eat," Misty Horn said hopefully.

"I'm not eating acorns!" Jada said, although her stomach was starting to rumble with hunger.

The Ohlone girl stepped forward. She stared at the three strangers.

"She must think that she's dreaming," Jada said.

The girl was startled by the odd syllables of English, but she didn't seem afraid.

"Maybe she has seen strangers like us," Ernesto wondered aloud.

"Maybe strangers come to her in dreams," Misty Horn said. "But they would only speak her language, Chochenyo."

The Ohlone girl pointed at their shoes.

"I guess she thinks they are baskets," Misty Horn said. "In *her* world, what else could they be?"

"Foot baskets," Jada mused.

"You're constantly *reading* the world. That's how you first learn. Your family and home are your first 'books.' When you come across something foreign or unfamiliar to your experience, you have to reevaluate. This girl is *reading* you into her world. That's what a Brazilian philosopher called it."

"When my parents came to Oakland, their world turned upside down. They lost their points of reference. It was hard for them to *read* the world," Ernesto said.

"I understand," Misty Horn said. "Where I grew up in Louisiana, I was told I was less than a white boy. That was the lesson I was never supposed to forget. After I came to California, I had to overcome what I'd been taught. I reeducated myself. I retook control of my destiny. That's why your parents brought you here. That's why they want you to stay in Oakland. They want you to determine your own destiny. Never forget that!"

The Ohlone girl shouted to the women beside the huts. She pointed to the strangers. They looked up and laughed. They didn't see anything unusual. After the girl gathered baskets with acorn flour and water, she motioned for the strangers to follow her.

They headed towards the bay and a huge shell-mound where clam, mussel, oyster, and abalone shells had been piled for centuries. At the shoreline were buoyant tule boats. The girl skipped up to a boat and pointed at the strangers. The men couldn't see them, but they laughed as they handed her a basket of clams.

"I'm not eating acorns," Jada repeated.

"You eat grits and posole," Misty Horn said.

"I love posole!" Ernesto replied.

Behind the shellmound, the Ohlone girl used a digging stick to make a shallow pit. Into the pit, she heaped dry leaves and twigs. On a hearth board, she swivelled a drill between her palms until the friction made a spark. A small fire blazed. Into the fire, the girl put a rock. When the rock was hot, she raised it with two sticks, cleaned it with a soaproot brush to remove the ashes, and placed it in a watertight basket with acorn meal and water. Instantly, the water began to boil.

"Cool!" Ernesto enthused.

"Col," the Ohlone girl mouthed.

"Of all the words, you have to teach her *cool!*" Jada chided.

"Co-ol," the girl tried again.

Ernesto pointed to himself. "ER-NES-TO."

"Nes-to," the girl laughed. "Hishmen."

"That's likely her name," Misty Horn said.

"Hishmen," Jada and Ernesto said.

The girl beamed. Never had dream strangers spoken her name. She stirred the acorn mush and dropped in the clams. It was time to eat.

The girl murmured in Chochenyo and gestured towards the food. Jada and Ernesto could not understand her words, but they recognized the meaning. Their families also knew that food was precious.

Using mussel shells as spoons, they ate from the exquisite basket. Even Jada liked it.

"I want to learn to cook like this," Ernesto said.

"Watertight baskets are rare," Misty Horn said. "You almost never see them except in museums."

"Maybe I can make one!"

"I can't really see you doing that!" Jada snickered.

"I might surprise you someday," Ernesto said.

Overhead the night was carpeted with tiny points of dazzling light. Jada could see more stars than on her camping trip with Maisha. She pointed to the North Star. Hishmen pointed, too. From a deerskin pouch, she picked out three abalone shells, cut and polished into pendants like small moons. She counted aloud as she put a pendant into each of their hands.

"Himhen, uTrin, kaphan," Hishmen said. She also showed them a string of shells with knots between them.

"The knots tell her how many days to the next festival," Misty Horn explained.

"I wish we had a gift," Jada said.

"You have a bracelet," Misty Horn hinted.

"It's not very special," Jada replied. "I got it at the 99 Cents store."

"It's special to Hishmen because it comes from you."

Jada removed the bangle from her arm. Ernesto took off his bandana. Hishmen turned them around in her hand. She smiled and slipped them into her deerskin pouch.

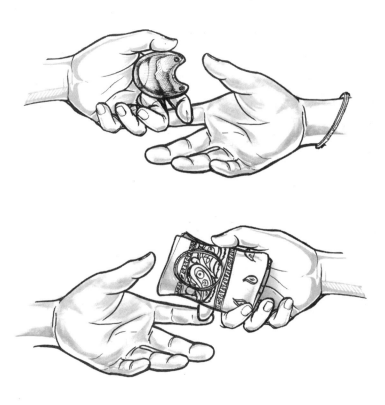

She picked out three abalone shells, cut and polished
into pendants like small moons.

"Maybe it's time to go," Jada said.

"As soon as the wind starts to blow, we'll go," Misty Horn promised.

Their Ohlone friend beckoned them again. They walked around the shellmound. Small waves lapped the rocky shore. Across the bay, the violet hills blended with the violet sky. It was difficult to see where the land stopped and the water began. They could see a gap in the hilly terrain where ships would someday sail into the San Francisco Bay. The gap would be known all over the world as the Golden Gate.

Jada and Ernesto had learned about the Ohlone in school, but it didn't make a deep impression. Now they could see the way life used to be. They gazed in disbelief. There were no bridges, no ships, no buildings, no electric lights.

"This is how Oakland once looked!" they said in awe.

They mounted a hill to a clearing. Whistles, rattles, clapper sticks, skin drums, and flutes made of reeds and bird bones resounded in the air. Men in feather headdresses and feather aprons, their bodies decorated with colored mud, snaked in a line. They shuffled in small steps, beating clapper sticks on their palms.

They curled and crouched as their heads and shoulders jerked in sharp movements.

"I hope the women do the acorn dance," Misty Horn said.

"I'd like to be an Aztec dancer," Ernesto said.

"Maybe after you finish your Ohlone basket?" Jada needled.

"All in good time," Misty Horn advised.

The drumming and clapping were soon muffled by the wind.

"It's our wind calling," Misty Horn said.

The wind rustled through the grass and whipped the feathers on the dancers' heads. Hair and clothes flapped as the wind grew stronger and wilder. Fog enveloped the village, the dancers, and the Ohlone girl as they faded from sight.

"Farewell, friend," Jada called.

"*Adiós*," Ernesto said.

At *Rancho Peralta*

"This isn't home!" Jada cried.

"Are we stuck?" Ernesto asked.

"Stuck!" Jada's eyes widened. "Does that happen?"

"Occasionally," Misty Horn said.

Ernesto surveyed the crest of the hills. "I can see a large herd of cattle up there."

Misty Horn looked up. "The Navigation Trees are still here."

"You mean they were cut down?" Jada asked.

"The biggest trees provided lumber to build early Oakland and early San Francisco. Hundreds of loggers lived in rough camps here in the hills. They say it sounded like thunder when the giant trees fell."

"I've got to get back!" Jada exclaimed. "I start Champions of Science on Tuesday!"

"Don't you have a fast-forward chant?" Ernesto suggested.

Misty Horn cupped his ear as music drifted through the woods. "Sounds like a *fandango* at the Peralta family ranch."

"Fan-dan-go?" Jada asked. It was the same word that the dancer inside the egg whispered in her ear.

"Picnics, rodeos, and races by day! Dancing and feasting at night! The Peraltas' parties are splendiferous!" Misty Horn's mouth watered for their *carne asada* and *chocolate caliente*.

"We're not dressed for a splen-di-fer-ous party!" Jada reminded them.

"We're travelers. We've journeyed farther than any other guest," Misty Horn winked. "No wonder we look so funny!"

They walked along the banks of Peralta Creek. Most of the thousands of acres of the Peraltas' *rancho* were open range for horses and cattle. Close to the living quarters were cultivated fields of pumpkins, onions, potatoes, cabbages, and wheat. Nearby were pear and apple orchards. There were also outbuildings that supported the necessities of daily life: stables, sheds, corrals, presses for olives and grapes, the blacksmith shop, and housing for the *vaqueros*. The Peraltas

Watercolor by Alfred Sully, c. 1849

lived in two adobe houses surrounded by an adobe
wall. The wall enclosed flower and vegetable gardens
and a *ramada*. This was the heart of the *hacienda*.

Through an arch in the wall, they stepped into
a pleasant courtyard. Along the interior of the wall
were lean-tos used for storage or makeshift beds for
overnight guests. A *ramada* had been constructed
with posts and beams. Leafy branches lay across the
beams to create a roof with no walls. At one end of the
ramada sat musicians with guitars, violins, and a harp.
At the other end gathered women, wearing silk shawls,
velvet dresses, and cameo brooches. As the music
began, the women lifted their voices in song.

"*Californios* love to sing and play music and eat rich food," Misty Horn laughed.

To get a better look, Jada peeked around the cool adobe wall. "A gentleman has walked into the center," she reported.

"That's our host, Don Antonio María Peralta," Misty Horn said.

"I like his high boots and silver spurs," Ernesto said. He also admired Don Antonio's black sombrero, embroidered jacket, and pants laced with ribbons.

The threesome watched as Don Antonio took off his hat, bowed, and stamped his foot in four directions. He stopped in front of a woman and clapped his hands.

"The dance is starting," Ernesto said.

"They are famous for dancing, too!"

Don Antonio led the woman into the center where they briefly danced. She went back to her chair. He led another woman into the center.

"I hope she doesn't trip on the fringes of her shawl," Jada said.

"After Don Antonio has introduced each woman, the dancing will begin," Misty Horn explained.

"She's lifting her ruffled petticoat off the floor," Jada said.

"She's showing off her ankles!" Misty Horn chortled.

"She looks African. Is that possible?"

"Many Afro-Latinos settled in *Alta California*. The last *Californio* governor, Pio Pico, was Afro-Latino."

"I never heard of Afro-Latino," Ernesto said.

"The Mexican Revolution abolished slavery decades before Lincoln's Emancipation Proclamation. Once Africans were free, they could move up the social ladder if they had money. There were many castes, many combinations of European, African, and Native blood."

Jada slapped Ernesto five. "Hey! You are my long-lost brother for real!"

CHAPTER

Bull versus Bear

Injustice anywhere is a threat to justice everywhere.
Martin Luther King, Jr.

After hours of dancing, a midnight supper of *cerdo asado* or roasted pig with onions, *arroz, pastel de frutas,* and *café* was served. Following more hours of dancing, a breakfast of *chile verde, frijoles, queso, tortillas,* and *fresas* was offered to the guests.

At first, Jada and Ernesto were too shy to dance. After Jada wrapped herself in a *rebozo* and Ernesto found a hat and a *serape,* they ventured into the circle of dancers. It took only a few missteps before they mastered the up-down-down, up-down-down of the waltz.

"These Mexicans sure know how to throw a *fandango!*" Ernesto exclaimed.

"Don't call them Mexicans! Or Spaniards!" Misty Horn said. "They are *Californios*! Don Antonio's father, Don Luís, traveled as a soldier in the king's army with the Anza expedition. From Mexico, they walked and rode horses and brought wagons with settlers and supplies. It took many months to reach *Alta California*."

"They walked?" Jada's legs ached from both walking and waltzing.

"Don Luís was rewarded with a bull, a cow, and a few acres."

"That's not much," Ernesto said.

"The bull and cow multiplied many times over. In 1820, Don Luís received a land grant of almost 45,000 acres where thousands of his cattle and horses grazed. The land stretched from San Leandro to El Cerrito and included Oakland. After Mexico won its independence from Spain, the new nation of Mexico plunged into chaos. The bad news was that supply ships to California stopped. The good news was that Spain and Mexico didn't patrol the California coast."

"What do you mean 'patrol'?" Ernesto asked.

"Now ships from other countries could come to Oakland to trade their goods. Suddenly ranchers like the Peraltas were free to exchange their cowhides and tallow on the worldwide market for special foods like coffee, sugar, and tea and products they did not make themselves like chinaware and cloth for their beautiful clothes. A cattle hide was known as a 'California dollar.' By the 1830s, the Peralta herds had grown to thousands of head of cattle and thousands of 'California dollars.' The Ohlones hauled the hides down what we call Thirteenth Avenue to the *embarcadero* and put them on ships in the estuary."

"One man with all that land and cattle?" Ernesto marveled.

"His four sons made good use of it."

"And the Ohlone?" Jada asked, suspecting the worst.

"Cows and horses trampled the meadows, ate the native grasses and seeds, and tore up the fragile roots with their hooves. How could the Ohlone maintain their way of life? The land was ruined and their lives altered forever. There were uprisings and rebellions, but . . . ," Misty Horn sighed heavily. "To survive, they went to the *ranchos,* the missions, and the *pueblos* where they did most of the work."

Jada touched the precious abalone pendant in her pocket. It would always remind her of their friend, Hishmen.

After breakfast, there was a wrestling match for the strongest lads. Ernesto was eager to join them, but Misty Horn cautioned, "We have to stay under the radar."

After the match, a *señorita* in a taffeta dress with a tortoise-shell comb and *mantilla* danced while a young man played guitar. The dancer reminded Ernesto of a Filipina girl he had liked in fifth grade. Inocencia's lively black eyes and long, wavy black hair were the same as the dancer's.

"Inocencia," he sighed her name.

Beneath the rose arbor, another party gathered to walk up into the hills for a picnic. Ohlone servants loaded a *carreta* with food and wine to take along.

Jada and Ernesto had never seen such extravagance: the clothes, the food, the horses and servants, and the dozens of guests.

"Do *Californios* hang out and kick it all day?" Jada asked.

"It's *fiesta* time now with lots of festivities," Misty Horn said. "Let's hope the wind picks up after the bullfight. Then we can be on our way."

Jada took a seat in the shade of the *ramada*. "No bullfight for me!"

Ohlone servant girls in muslin shifts scurried by. Gone were the feathers, shells, and tule skirts. None of them had tattoos. Their ease and joy had drained away.

"*Buenos días,*" an Ohlone girl spoke to Jada.

"*Buenos días,*" Jada replied, pulling out her abalone pendant.

The Ohlone girl turned it over in her palm. The pendant resembled a small, iridescent moon. She touched Jada's pants and shoes and hair. The clothes made her look boyish, but she had a girl's voice and face. "*Africana?*" the Ohlone asked.

"*Sí, Africana,*" Jada said.

From the bullring, they heard flutes and drums and cheers. The girl lowered her head like a bull and struck her chest with her fists like a bear.

"*Toro y oso,*" she cried.

"Bull and bear?" Jada repeated in disbelief.

She took Jada's hand and led her behind the adobe houses. As they came closer to the bullring, Jada's hand tightened. Brutality frightened her. She once saw a man shot in Raimondi Park. Another time, there was a gunfight next to her house. She had nightmares about street violence.

When they reached the corral for the bullfights, they found a makeshift viewing platform on the outside of the fence where they could sit. Inside the corral, dust swirled as horsemen raced around the ring. The horses were covered with thick, decorative pads, their manes and tails braided with ribbons and bells, their saddles constructed of inlaid wood with tooled leather and tipped with silver.

At a signal from Don Antonio, a gate was lifted. Snorting with rage, a bull stampeded into the corral and rushed the horses. Within seconds, a rider had been thrown to the ground and his horse gouged.

"Oh, no!" Jada shrieked.

After the bull was driven back through the gate, the *toro y oso* were led into the corral. Handlers held the animals with long *reatas* and paraded them around. The crowd cheered and jeered. Those standing beside the fence tossed flowers, sombreros, gold and silver coins, and boots into the corral.

The bear and bull did not react. They simply let themselves be led. Finally, they were staked in the center of the ring. The back foot of the grizzly bear was tied to the front foot of the bull.

The spectators discussed which animal would be victorious. The bull with his sharp horns? Or the bear with his deadly claws? The animals displayed no hostility until the *vaqueros* hit them with sticks and whips.

The bear growled as he tried to dislodge his foot. The bull grunted as he shook his leg in frustration.

"You don't look like you're enjoying yourself," a young man said to Jada in English.

"Not much," she nodded as she watched with horror and fascination. She wasn't sure whether to stay or flee. She looked around for Ernesto and Misty Horn, but they were nowhere in sight.

"We *Californios* love the spectacle of the bullfight: the horses, the pageantry, the danger, the swordsmanship," the young man said. "It's our Spanish heritage."

"Are you a *Californio*?" she asked, regarding his rosy face and his waxed mustache. He didn't look *Californio*.

"This is my adopted country," he said. "I live in Yerba Buena across the bay. I sailed over yesterday for the Peraltas' party."

Jada stared at the bullring. "It's too cruel," she said.

"There are aspects of cruelty like life itself. Perhaps you're too young to understand."

"I understand!" Jada cried. She'd witnessed cruelty at school and in the streets.

"*¡Vamos!*" the crowd yelled impatiently. They were tired of waiting.

Jada stared even harder. She couldn't believe what she saw. Ernesto had squeezed between two fence posts and staggered into the ring.

"Ernesto! Ernesto!" she called.

She took out her phone and tapped several buttons. Then she remembered Ernesto didn't have a phone. What was she thinking? Telephones hadn't been invented!

"STOP!" Ernesto shouted.

The astonished crowd turned to each other with questions. Ernesto's saggy, baggy pants, the bulky white leather shoes, and the baseball hat must have looked ridiculous to them.

"STOP!" Ernesto shouted again. His voice was loud and shrill.

The crowd grew silent. They forgot about the bull and bear. All eyes were on the young man.

Many thoughts collided in Ernesto's mind. He had been so proud of the *Californios*. After all, they were originally Mexican like himself. They lived on this land many decades before other Europeans. They traveled through the same desert and difficult terrain that his parents traveled to reach *Alta California*. Like the Peraltas, Ernesto wanted to be dashing and generous. He wanted to give his parents things they never had. However, as he observed their world, Ernesto's thoughts became confused.

"*¡Tranquilo! ¡Tranquilo!*" he mumbled, walking towards the bull's foaming snout and the bear's ferocious teeth.

"*¡No!*" the people cringed.

Ernesto was oblivious to their cries. Instead he saw the animals' fear. He saw the fear of the Ohlones who'd been uprooted from their world. He saw the faces of his dead friend, Freddy, and his wounded friend, Paco, along with the Oakland streets of gangs, guns, cops, courts, and jail. Most of all, he saw his *madre* and *padre* who'd been treated unjustly.

When Ernesto understood what he saw, he had to try to stop it. *Somebody has to try*, he told himself. *Why not Ernesto Cruz?*

Jada ran to the fence. "That's my brother! Let me in!" she cried.

The *vaqueros* studied her African-American face, her cargo pants, her crazy shoes, and her air of desperation.

"*¡Es mi hermano! ¡Abre la puerta!*" she begged.

Then without warning, a terrific wind blew around them. As fierce as a tornado, the wind tossed men's hats and lifted ladies' skirts. It stirred the dust into billowing brown clouds. It bent the limbs of trees. Dogs barked. Children screamed. Horses stomped and reared. The bear and bull were so frantic that they broke the *reatas* around their feet. With the bull and bear loose, pandemonium erupted everywhere.

"Ernesto! Jada! Come quickly! It's our wind!"

By the Lake and on the Bay

Ernesto lay on a grassy bank beside Lake Merritt, his eyes closed, and his lips quivering. "*¡Tranquilo! ¡Tranquilo!*" he muttered.

Jada held his hand. Misty Horn mopped his forehead with a handkerchief.

Surrounding the lake were mansions and boat docks, private tennis courts and gardens. Flocks of ducks, geese, and swans glided over the water. Other birds nested at the marshy edge. It was a different Lake Merritt: no Fairyland or Pergola or Colonnade, no apartment houses or traffic.

"Should we call an ambulance?" Jada asked.

"I doubt the servants in these houses would let two colored people use their telephone," Misty Horn said. "As for public phones, they don't exist."

Jada pointed across the lake to a huge white building with a small cupola on top. "Is that a hospital?"

"It's a convent and will soon become a college," Misty Horn said. "The public hospitals, Fabiola and Providence, are located more than ten blocks away."

"No phones, no ambulances, no 9-1-1?" Jada asked.

"These large houses have chauffeurs and horseless carriages, but would they take us to a hospital?"

"I guess not," she said with resignation. Out of place and out of time, who would help them?

Skipping along the bank of the lake was a youth dressed in torn knickers and a stained jacket. His scuffed boots flopped over his shins. Between the boots and knickers were his skinned, scabby legs.

He stopped beside Ernesto. "Is he okay?" he asked.

"We're not sure," Misty Horn said.

"I've got something," he said, reaching into his knickers and lifting out a small bottle. "Chinamen have all kinds of medicines."

The boy uncorked the bottle and sprinkled a few granules of smelling salts under Ernesto's nose.

Ernesto stirred. His eyes blinked. "*¡Mamá! ¡Mamá!*" he babbled.

"That did the trick," the boy said, plugging the cork back in the bottle.

Ernesto sat up and rubbed his eyes. "Lake Merritt!"

"You've got that right!" The boy shook Ernesto's hand. "I guess my salts fixed you up."

"Did I faint?" Ernesto asked, recalling the Peraltas' bullring.

"You're better now," Jada said.

"Hey, you're a girl?" the boy asked, looking up and down at Jada's pants.

"I'm a girl," Jada replied, insulted by the question.

"I've never seen a girl wear pants."

"But girls wear . . . ," Jada hesitated. She wasn't sure what to say.

"She borrowed them from her brother," Misty Horn explained.

"I didn't think you were girl, but now that I see you good, you sure look like a girl," the boy said. "By golly, I'm out here playing hooky. You aren't telling on me, are you?"

"I've played hooky once or twice," Ernesto smiled.

"Me too," Jada admitted.

"How come you're missing work today?" the boy asked.

"Work? I'm too young to work!" Jada exclaimed.

"You don't look too young," the boy observed.

"I work in a restaurant," Ernesto said.

"Sometimes I babysit," Jada said. After she turned fourteen, she hoped to get a real job. One of Jada's friends worked in a community garden on weekends. Another was learning to cook at a restaurant.

"Once in a while," the boy said dreamily, "I've got to go outside in the fresh air even if I get a beating."

Jada noticed the red splotches on the boy's face and the dark circles under his eyes. "Kids our age don't have to work," she said. "It's against the law."

"Law? All my kind work in the mills or laundries or canneries, down at the docks, or in the rail yards. If you want to eat, you've got to work."

"When do you go to school?" Ernesto asked.

"Some poor kids go to school. Even colored kids go to school. Rich kids go to school every day and college, too. But I stay in the blasted cotton mill twelve hours a day and six days a week. If I'm not working, I'm sleeping. My schooling days are behind me." The boy tapped his head. "A mill is the loudest place you'll hear in your whole life. Dust always gets caught in your throat and lungs. The heat is infernal. Most everybody dies of brown-lung disease. April 17 is different. It's my thirteenth birthday. That's why I'm playing hooky. What's your excuse?"

Except for a line of fuzz over his lips, he didn't look thirteen. He barely looked ten. He was scrawny and thin. His shoulders stooped. His cheeks sank into his bony face. His knickers and jacket were too small, his cap too big.

"I guess we don't have an excuse," Ernesto said.

Jada hummed "Happy Birthday" as Ernesto sang.

"What's the year?" Misty Horn interrupted.

"You don't know what year it is?" the boy asked.

"It's not 1906, is it?" Misty Horn said anxiously.

"That's exactly right!" the boy shouted.

Misty Horn closed his eyes and chanted:

The harder we look, the more we see!
The more we stare, the sooner we get there!

He waited for a wild wind to blow, but nothing happened.

"Blow!" he groaned under his breath.

"Shucks!" the boy said. "Since you're already playing hooky, do you want to celebrate with Joãozinho?"

"Jo-zo-ho what?" Jada stumbled over the syllables.

"That's my Portuguese name, but they call me Johnny."

Ernesto pumped Johnny's hand. "I'm Ernesto. This is Jada and our traveling companion, Misty Horn."

Johnny grinned broadly, displaying two rows of crooked yellow teeth and holes where his cuspids were missing.

"Do you live over in Jingletown?" Misty Horn asked.

"Yes siree! Jingletown is the place to be!"

"We've still got Jingletown," Ernesto said.

"Of course, we've got it!" Johnny said. "Since the Portuguese moved in, we walk around jingling coins in our pockets. I make $2.40 a week as a doffer. My sisters make the same at the cannery. They come home half-deaf from the noise and stinking of peaches. You think peach might be nice. It's not! We give all our jingle to *papai*. If I bring home $2.30, he beats me for a dime. That's my *papai*."

"He doesn't sound like a very nice man," Jada blurted.

"After the scabs beat him up in the railroad strike, he went half-looney. He lost his arm helping to dig the channel that cut Alameda off from Oakland." Johnny smiled as if he didn't have a care in the world. "You've just got to understand him."

"Does your mother understand him?" Jada probed.

128

"My mother died," he said.

"Before you ask me about workers' comp and child labor laws, forget it," Misty Horn said. "Most workers don't have eight-hour days. Or sick leave. Or paid vacations."

Jada knew about unions. Her mother was in the Amalgamated Transit Union Local 192. The union protected bus drivers' rights. In Oakland, Ernesto's mother had worked ten hours a day in a tortilla factory. The boss only paid her for six. For an immigrant, a bad job was better than no job.

Johnny and his new friends sat enjoying the mild weather, the view of the rowboats on the lake, and the fits and starts of the horseless carriages riding over the macadam roads.

"Here come those swell ladies again!" Johnny announced. "I wish the twins could go up the hill and live in one of those swell orphan cottages. I've seen them. They've got a piano and everything. You eat plenty and go to school, too."

Marching towards them was a group of women in long, beautiful dresses, lace gloves, ornate hats, and leather shoes tied with silk ribbons. All the finery was coordinated in the colors of the suffrage campaign – white, gold, and purple – with pins, buttons, sashes, banners, and flags that read: **WOMEN'S RIGHT TO VOTE!**

"*Papai* says voting never helped workingmen. Why should it help ladies?"

"You mean women can't vote?" Jada asked indignantly.

Johnny rolled his eyes. "Where are you from?"

"Like I said, we're a little out of touch," Misty Horn interjected.

"I'll say!"

"They're suffragettes," Misty Horn said. "They've been fighting to vote for decades."

"We have one of those banners in our attic," Jada said, marveling at the silk dresses and enormous hats. "Are suffragettes all rich and white?"

"That's a touchy subject," Misty Horn said. "Some suffragettes want to include Negro women. Others do not. They worry that the issue of race will get confused with voting."

Ernesto stared at the impressive feathered hats. "Lots of birds died to make those hats," he said. "I thought you told us Lake Merritt was the first wildlife sanctuary in the whole United States!"

"Feathered hats were the fashion," Misty Horn said. "Across the country, millions of birds were slaughtered every year for hats."

The ladies marched past en route to City Hall.

"Women really can't vote?" Jada asked again.

"In California, women will win the vote sooner than most places," Misty Horn said.

"We want to help celebrate your birthday," Ernesto suggested. "I've got a few quarters."

"I've got a dollar in jingle," Jada added.

Johnny squealed with delight. "I'm planning to go out on the water. If you want, you can come, too."

Ernesto nodded at Misty Horn. "It depends on what he says."

"He's not your *papai*, is he? She's not your sister, is she?"

"She's like my sister," Ernesto affirmed.

"Okay by me," Johnny said. "They tell us that Chinamen and colored people are the lowest on the ladder, but I don't have anything against anybody."

"I thought Indians were the lowest," Ernesto said.

"I never saw an Indian," Johnny confessed. "But there's nothing lower than a Chinaman."

"That's not true now," Jada said.

"It's true as true," Johnny protested. "Mongolians aren't citizens. They can't vote or marry somebody that isn't Chinese. They have to go to separate schools. Some places they won't even let them walk on the sidewalk. They're treated real bad."

"Like blacks in the Jim Crow South," Misty Horn sighed. "Here in Oakland, it was very difficult for Asians and blacks to borrow money from banks and to buy property. Restrictive covenants and later redlining guaranteed that only whites lived in certain neighborhoods."

"I've got a good friend, Mr. Yuen. He's a Chinaman. His cousin works with me in the mill. That's how we got to be friends. I'm off to ask if he'll lend me his sampan. Come on!"

Johnny jogged down Webster to Ninth Street. Jada, Ernesto, and even Misty Horn jogged behind him. Jostling past were Chinese women and men, some in traditional robes with a skullcap or *baó*. Others were dressed in Western clothing with tailored jackets, trousers, bowler hats, and watch chains dangling from their waistcoats. Moving more slowly were Chinese vendors with long poles slung over their shoulders and baskets filled with fresh vegetables at each end of the pole. Piled on carts and in food stalls were dried fish and shrimp, mussels and crabs, dried mushrooms, ginseng roots, noodles, taro, and pressed ducks. Signs in Chinese characters hung above doors to indicate grocers, herbalists, restaurants, laundries, and tongs. Everywhere were stacks of wooden crates and boxes. Wafting through the air were the delicate sounds of the *erhu* and the delectable smells of sesame oil and fried noodles.

Johnny stopped in front of a narrow brick building.

"Mr. Yuen!" he yelled up to the second-floor balcony. Then he turned to his new friends, "Mr. Yuen cooks over at a Bella Vista mansion. It has fifteen bedrooms, a Chinese cook, a Japanese gardener, two French maids, and four Irish cleaning girls. Isn't that the life?"

"Where's Bella Vista?" Jada asked.

"Up Hopkins Street near Fourth Avenue," Johnny said.

"Where's Hopkins Street?" Ernesto asked.

Misty Horn whispered, "Hopkins Street is what we call MacArthur Boulevard. Fourth Avenue is Park Boulevard."

"It's east of the lake," Johnny said. "Have you been there?"

"We really don't know where anything is," Jada admitted.

A glass door opened. Jasmine incense floated through the air. Mr. Yuen was dressed in a boxy black jacket and loose silk pants. On his head was a black *baó*. A long queue hung down his back.

"It's early, Johnny," Mr. Yuen complained.

"I was telling my new friends about Fruit Vale. They've got orchards and nurseries, berry farms and dairies, resort hotels and German beer gardens. You've never seen such pretty places."

"What happened to the Peraltas' rancho?" Ernesto asked Misty Horn. "I thought they owned all the land."

"Americans stole, speculated, and squatted on whatever Peralta land they found. You see, the Peraltas didn't have money in the bank. Their wealth was land, cattle, and hides known as 'California dollars.' They had to fight in court to hold onto their land. Most of it was lost. When Antonio Peralta died, he owned only his house on Thirty-Fourth Avenue and a couple dozen acres."

"And the Ohlone?"

"Things got worse when the Americans began moving west into California during the Gold Rush. They pushed the Natives off the land and often killed them. To survive, Ohlones started claiming to be something else."

Mr. Yuen called down from the balcony. "Are you playing hooky, Johnny?"

"If I bring you a bushel of clams, can I take out the sampan, Mr. Yuen?"

Mr. Yuen waved his cigarette holder. "More than a bushel," he said.

"We're going to Goat Island for my birthday," Johnny explained.

"Three bushels," Mr. Yuen said, throwing down a handful of salted plums wrapped in a sheet of a Chinese newspaper. "Happy birthday, Johnny!"

Johnny led them on a quick tour of downtown Oakland. Tracks lay in the middle of the streets for trains and electric streetcars: local service for the Key Route system plus the transcontinental railroad lines that traveled across the United States to reach Oakland.

They passed the city's first skyscraper, at Thirteenth and Broadway, saw the suffragettes protesting on the steps of City Hall, past the Oakland Free Public Library at Fourteenth and Grove, and over to the observatory at Eleventh and Jefferson.

"It's the original Chabot Observatory," Misty Horn said. "When they moved to the Oakland hills where the nights were darker, they took the telescopes inside these domes with them."

"Can we look?" Jada asked expectantly.

"We don't have time today," Johnny said. "We've got to sail with the tide."

The markets on Lower Washington Street were filled with shoppers buying fruit, meat, fresh bread, vegetables, and sweets. Johnny's mouth began to water. For two weeks, he'd eaten only crackers and lupin beans.

He pointed at the Italian deli. "I'll be back in a minute!"

From the deli's ceiling hung cured sausages and salamis. Large crockery jars brimmed with pickles and olives. Bags of dry cannellini beans and large tins of olive oil sat on the floor. Barrels with different shapes of pasta stood against the walls. Behind a glass case were sliced meats, mozzarella cheese, and cakes.

Many of Oakland's Italian families had moved to Temescal, but some still lived in West Oakland. Johnny had almost no trouble making himself understood. Since he spoke Portuguese, he could understand some Italian. He also knew bits of German and Chinese.

He bought four sour pickles, a hard salami, sour-dough rolls, a hunk of cheese, and a bottle of mineral water. For dessert, he filled a bag with penny candy.

Johnny led them across the tracks and past the train station at Seventh Street and Broadway. Thundering around them were the grating noises of whistles, horns, and brakes; the commotion of passengers getting on and off trains; the shouts of luggage handlers hauling carts; streetcars clanging past; and the cries of street vendors selling food. Steam hissed, machines hummed, and men shouted. As they approached the shoreline, the pungent smells of creosote and burning coal filled the air. The waterfront was just as busy with ships, ferries, cranes, docks, sailors, longshoremen, stevedores, saloons, boardinghouses, and cheap hotels. Oakland was raw and vibrant, pulsing with colorful sites and people.

Johnny located Mr. Yuen's sampan on the estuary. He clambered over the rock wall that lined the shore.

"Isn't it a beauty?" he cried.

"It's small," Jada said cautiously.

"You think we can fit?" Ernesto asked.

"Sure as sure. You can't move up, down, around, or we might tip over."

"I'm not a good swimmer," Jada said.

137

"You can wear this thing." Johnny handed Jada a vest made of corks and held together by twine. "Mr. Yuen says if you've got this on, you won't drown."

"Do you know how to handle a sampan on the rough bay?" Misty Horn asked.

"Shucks!" Johnny boasted. "I've done it a thousand times!"

They climbed in. Johnny stood in the stern with a single oar that fit through a hole in the deck. He used the oar to steer the boat. Ernesto balanced on the gunwale near the bow. Jada and Misty Horn sat on a bench behind a curved mat roof.

Johnny maneuvered the sampan around schooners, steamboats, barges, large ferries, and whalers. As they moved out towards San Francisco Bay, they looked at the shore of West Oakland. Typhoid, malaria from mosquitos, sewage, and millions of flies made life near the marsh unhealthy.

"That's the top of my house!" Jada shouted.

"I didn't know you were *rich*," Johnny said. He lived in a two-room carriage house with his *papai*, older sisters, and young twins. "I bet you even go to school!"

"I'm not rich. My great-great-grandpa only made a few cents a day as a Pullman porter."

"Plus good tips and respect!" Misty Horn added.

"Joseph Russell must be living there now," Jada said excitedly.

"Talking to family members is tricky," Misty Horn whispered to Jada. "Mr. Russell is the bloodline from his time to yours. You could get stuck and never get back to your time."

"What if we walk by the house and I promise not to say a word?"

"We might be able to do that," Misty Horn conceded.

At the outer limits of the harbor, Johnny attached a slanted sail to the mast. They gazed across the water. Jada had visited San Francisco three or four times. Ernesto had never been there. Neither had ever been in a boat.

As soon as the wind billowed in the sail, the sampan sped along. The cold, choppy waves sprayed their faces and hair with saltwater. Porpoises frolicked beside the boat. It felt as if they were flying. It felt like they might sail into the sky.

"If you think this is fast," Johnny yelled over the wind, "Mr. Yuen has a friend, Feng Ru, who is building himself a flying machine! Is that the craziest thing you ever heard?"

"You mean an airplane?" Ernesto said.

"I don't know what the heck they call it!"

Jada pointed to a long pier that jutted into water. "What's that?"

"You live over yonder and never saw a mole?"

Jutting into the bay were long piers with tracks. One belonged to the Southern Pacific Railroad and the other to the Key Route system. Trains rolled over the moles for miles into the water where passengers boarded ferries to take them to San Francisco. Some Southern Pacific ferries were the biggest in the world, large enough to transport multiple train cars.

"There's no bridge!" Ernesto hollered.

"How are they going to build a bridge to Goat Island?" Johnny hollered back. "It's too far!"

Jada leaned into Misty Horn's ear. "Where's Goat Island?" she asked.

"It was first called Yerba Buena Island, then changed to Goat Island, and then Yerba Buena again," he said.

Once they neared the island, Johnny lowered the sail and guided them to shore. He unfastened his high boots and removed the soggy cardboard in the soles.

"Guess the cardboard got ruined," he said, inspecting the holes in the bottom of his shoes.

"You can have my socks," Ernesto said.

It felt as if they were flying. It felt like they might sail into the sky.

"Socks is the best birthday present I ever got!"

As the sampan touched sand, Johnny jumped from the stern into shallow water. Jada, Ernesto, and Misty Horn took off their shoes and waded in the water, too. It was cold and exhilarating.

"I reckon we can sit here and eat," Johnny said as he rolled up his knickers. "After lunch, I've got to take a bath."

Jada was surprised. "They have bathrooms?"

"Bathrooms? You must be rich! I'm talking about a cove where we can get naked."

"No, thanks!" Jada said.

"I can't wait to wash off," Ernesto said. "I guess I haven't bathed in . . . ."

"A few hundred years!" Misty Horn laughed.

After lunch, Ernesto and Johnny began to tussle. They threw each other on the sand. Soon they were sparring. Johnny was small and wiry and undernourished, but he was strong.

"You're a pretty good boxer," Johnny said.

"You're pretty good, too."

"I'm more than pretty good! I'm a scrapper!" Johnny gloated. "I plan to box my way to the top. That's the only way I'll ever get out of the mill."

Ernesto brushed the sand off his clothes. "Let's take that cold dip."

"Maybe Jada wants to dig for clams while we wash up," Johnny said.

"I don't know how," she said.

Johnny lifted a stick and poked it in the wet sand. "There's one!" He poked the stick again. "There's another!"

The afternoon passed quickly. Too soon, they climbed in the sampan with the buckets of clams, raised the sail, and started back to Oakland.

"We don't know how to thank you," Jada said.

"Shucks! We had a swell time!" Johnny glowed.

"Sailing with you was the coolest thing I ever did," Ernesto said.

"Cool?" Johnny puzzled.

"Happy birthday!" they sang.

"Shucks!" Johnny said. "This is the best birthday of my whole life."

Whole Lotta Shakin' Goin' On

"I guess I'll go home and take my lumps," Johnny said.

Misty Horn reached inside his pocket. "Here's a silver dollar that you can give to your *papai*. Maybe he won't be so harsh."

"Golly, Mr. Horn! You're giving me a whole dollar for doing nothing!"

"Here's two more dollars to keep for yourself. If you go back to school, you'll need supplies."

Johnny jumped up and down. "I can't tell you how much this means to me, Mr. Horn!"

"Now run along so your *papai* doesn't find another reason to get mad."

An exuberant Johnny grinned and shook hands with Misty Horn and Ernesto.

"See you in the ring!" he winked and raised his fists.

"You've got to stay a step ahead, that's what my coach says," Ernesto advised. "It's your best defense."

Johnny waved as he ran off. They waved after him.

"I guess we'll never see him again," Jada sighed.

They turned down Seventh Street towards West Oakland. Missing were freeways, parking lots, and BART. Traffic was horse- or mule-drawn buggies and wagons. When they passed the West Oakland Free Reading Room, Jada's heart raced faster. The neighborhood was both the same and different. Oak trees lined the macadam street. Scattered among the Queen Anne cottages were commercial establishments: a barbershop, an icehouse, a cobbler, saloons and corner markets, the butcher and smokehouse, a blacksmith, and a horse stable.

"I guess they don't believe in cleaning up," Ernesto said, observing the mounds of manure.

"They believe!" Misty Horn chuckled. "In downtown, manure constantly gets hauled away. Here in West Oakland, it's a chronic problem."

Jada held her nose. "It smells," she said.

"That's one reason why folks welcomed the automobile. Unfortunately, gasoline smells, too."

Jada skipped down the street and stopped in front of her house. The sprawling rosebush was only a sprout. On the steps, a stout woman was busily sweeping. She swept the steps and continued down the walkway to the road.

"Good afternoon," she said cheerfully.

"Good afternoon," Misty Horn replied.

She turned to Ernesto and Jada. "Good afternoon to you."

"Good afternoon," they said.

Jada recognized the woman as Alvina Chester Russell, wife of her great-great-uncle Jeremiah Russell. Her photograph hung in the hall of the house next to the grandfather clock. Jada stared at Mrs. Russell's plump, fresh face. Her hair was braided and bundled at the back of her neck. She wore a stiffly starched white blouse tucked into a long gray skirt and high-button lavender shoes.

"My, my! You must be strangers in these parts!" she said graciously. "Let me fetch you a glass of lemonade. I picked the lemons this morning."

Misty Horn said graciously in return, "We thank you kindly."

"You looking for beds to rent?" Alvina Russell asked.

As Jada started to speak, Misty Horn restrained her. "No, ma'am, we're only passing through."

"We have a couple of vacancies in the attic."

"Attic?" Jada darted towards the door.

"Men only," Mrs. Russell said. "I can put the girl on the second floor. Rooms include board. Anyone will tell you the Russells run the cleanest house in West Oakland. We mostly rent to railroad men. You don't strike me as a Pullman porter."

"No, ma'am," Misty Horn said. "I do admire our porters. They've done so much to advance the Negro cause. They carry the news, good and bad, wherever they go. Without them, I'm afraid we wouldn't know half as much about what's going on across the country."

"Amen!" Alvina Russell said. "You'd like my brother-in-law, Joseph Russell. He's very active in the cause of Negro rights. Of course, he understands that no amount of self-improvement on *our* part can totally overcome prejudice on *their* part."

Jada interrupted, "Can we meet Mr. Russell?"

Misty Horn signaled a warning to Jada. Then he hastened to say, "We don't have time to meet him!"

"He left for Chicago early this morning," Alvina Russell said. "Joe only has Jeremiah and me since his wife passed away."

Jada's face turned thoughtful and sad.

"What a sweet girl! She's sad over someone she never met!" Alvina said.

Jada wiped her eyes. "I feel like I've met her."

Misty Horn explained, "Jada feels connected to the past in all sorts of ways."

"That's a good thing, but we've got to look to the future for change," Mrs. Russell said. She turned to Ernesto, "What about you, young man?"

"I miss my family in Mexico."

"You tell them to come right up to Oakland," she insisted. "The train companies hire Mexicans all the time."

"I'm afraid it isn't easy," Ernesto said.

"It's easy as pie," she said.

Two trains passed each other on Seventh Street. Horns blared and brakes screeched.

"If you live here, you get used to the noise," Mrs. Russell said.

"I've never gotten used to it," Jada replied.

"If this young man wants to meet Mexicans, I can introduce him to my friends the Sandoval family."

"We appreciate your courtesy," Misty Horn said politely. "We've got to be going."

"Next time, I hope you can linger in West Oakland. It's a delightful place to be. We have the best weather anywhere."

After they bid farewell to Alvina Russell, they walked towards Sixteenth Street. Sammy's Sugar Shack stood on the corner, its menu scrawled on a blackboard that leaned against the door:

GUMBO!
CAJUN chicken!
Red Beans & Rice!
Collards!
Biscuits!
Cherry Cobbler!

Jada looked across the street at the wooden building with trains, porters, luggage carts and passengers. "What happened to the big station?"

"The beautiful Southern Pacific station hasn't been built yet."

"I guess things change," Jada reflected.

"Are you *just* realizing that?" Ernesto chided.

A voice called out from Sammy's Sugar Shack, "Good evening!"

"Good afternoon!" Misty Horn called back.

"Whatever time it is, come feast on the best cooking west of Chicago!"

An ancient man stepped forward. He was short and bony. His parchment-thin skin was the color of tar. His black eyes were buried in a wrinkled face. His wooden false teeth were held in his mouth with a gold metal ring. There were deep scars on his neck and arms.

"I'm Sammy!" he said cordially. "This is my shack!"

"Quite a nice shack," Misty Horn said, regarding Sammy's checkered apron and chef's toque, the linen tablecloths and napkins, and recent copies of *The Oakland Sunshine* and *Western Outlook*, two of the local black newspapers.

"Seat yo'self anywhere!" Sammy waved while he went to fetch three bowls of gumbo.

"Takes me home to Louisiana!" Misty Horn declared.

"When y'all cook like home, y'all bring home wherever y'all go," Sammy said.

"So, where is home?"

"Home is wherever the heart roams," Sammy said, taking off his toque and rubbing his bald black head.

"If I told y'all I was born a slave on the Sheffield plantation, y'all believe me?"

"A slave!" Jada and Ernesto gasped.

"I was a sickly pup so they put me to work with Momma in the kitchen."

"You learned well," Misty Horn smiled with satisfaction. "Did you come to California after the Civil War?"

"Master Sheffield brought me during the Gold Rush. Master hated to miss a good meal. In the gold camps, I not only cooked for him. Others paid me to cook and wash their laundry. I worked triple-time until I got enough dollars to buy my freedom."

"Many blacks came to California as slaves," Misty Horn said.

"Y'all could try to escape or buy yo' freedom. Escape was dangerous. If you were a fugitive slave and they tracked you down, they hauled y'all back. Unless y'all run away to Indian peoples. Down South, Indians hid us in the swamp. That's how we got so many 'black Indians' around New Orleans. When I left Master Sheffield, he told me I graduated from three-fifths to one whole person. Freedom cost me two thousand dollars. I figured one thousand each for the other two-fifths of me. I was still afraid. Even with freedom papers, Negroes wasn't safe. I stayed fearful until after the Civil War."

Ernesto thought about his parents. A piece of paper could decide if you were free or not, legal or illegal, "alien" or not.

"I bought my brother and sister's freedom, too," Sammy said. "More than a thousand apiece!"

"A fortune!" Jada exclaimed.

"Can y'all name me a thing more precious than freedom? Freedom fulfilled my whole life. Next time y'all come this way and don't find Sammy's Sugar Shack, look for me at the Home for Colored People over in Beulah."

When they left Sammy, it was twilight. They walked by West Oakland's marsh. As it grew dark, they stumbled past the De Fremery mansion and blocks of small houses until they reached the streetcar that took them north to Fifty-Sixth Street and Idora Park.

Inside the park was a wonderland: a roller-skating rink, a theater, a stadium for the Oakland Oaks baseball team, a penny arcade, an artificial mountain, a scenic railroad, and the biggest roller coaster in the entire United States!

"I wish we still had Idora Park," Ernesto said, gazing around in awe.

Idora Park, North Oakland

"We have Fairyland!" Misty Horn said.

"Fairyland is for little kids." Jada grumbled.

"They say it was Walt Disney's inspiration."

"I've never been to Fairyland or Disneyland," Ernesto said.

"You've been to Idora Park! None of your friends can claim that!"

Throughout the evening, Misty Horn silently repeated his mantra:

The harder we look, the more we see!
The more we stare, the sooner we get there!

He hoped the wind would sweep them forward in time, but his hopes were dashed. At dawn on April 18, 1906, calamity struck. All around them, the earth rocked. Buildings fell. Roofs collapsed. Windows shattered. Chimneys toppled. Many streets and tracks buckled. Water mains and gas lines broke. Fires erupted. There were shrieks and screams as men, women, and children swarmed into the streets. The shock lasted an eternal forty-two seconds.

Jada cried, "Has everything fallen down?"

Misty Horn tried to calm them. "Oakland has suffered. However, most of the damage is in San Francisco, both from earthquake and fire."

"I want to go home," Jada whimpered. All she wanted was to crawl into her mother's lap.

"I'm doing my best, but I can't seem to move us forward," Misty Horn said meekly. "Meanwhile, with people and animals buried, injured, hungry, and cold, we won't lack for things to do."

All day folks poured into Idora Park. Some brought tents, blankets, pots, pans, and food. Most brought nothing. Soon there was a large campground. First-aid stations were established. Tent kitchens sprang up.

A pale, bony woman with a gaunt face, freckled skin, tiny bright blue eyes, smudges of soot on her cheeks and nightshirt, and bits of rubble in her red hair, pointed to Jada and Ernesto. "You two colored kids, get over here!"

Jada bristled. "*Colored* makes me squirm," she said to Ernesto.

"I guess it's the times," he said.

Nevertheless, they stepped forward to help. Kathleen put them to work chopping carrots, slicing onions, and peeling potatoes. Soon they were preparing pots of savory vegetable stew and porridge and ladling portions into empty tin cans. Whoever was hungry had plenty to eat. No money was needed. For the frightened children, there was not only food but also storytellers and musicians who did their part to entertain them. In spite of the terror and hardship and injuries, people laughed and sang and played music. It was a celebration of survival. Misty Horn called it "civil society at its best."

Once Jada started to help, she couldn't stop smiling. She was no longer afraid. She no longer thought about home. She was happy. "Colored" or not, she had never felt so useful in her life. She now knew what it meant to have a purpose. Everyone was a new friend, including Kathleen.

The sky was dark and smoky from the burning city across the San Francisco Bay. Jada and Ernesto were recruited to a nearby bakery where they rapidly learned to make bread. The loaves they baked were sent by ferry to San Francisco. For a week, Oakland delivered a hundred thousand loaves of bread every day across the bay. Huge crowds of men, women, and children were ferried to Oakland. Tens of thousands would find refuge in Oakland's tent camps, churches, factories, and private homes. Many would make Oakland their permanent home.

After the baking was finished, they boarded a streetcar to West Oakland. Trains and streetcars were free. Drivers worked through the night and into the next day. Everybody pitched in to help.

They first checked on Sammy and his shack. Half a wall had fallen down, the windows were cracked, and his stove had been dragged to the sidewalk. Like others they met, Sammy was smiling and singing as he stirred his cast-iron pots.

"Hello, my traveling friends!" he greeted them. "I guess y'all come back!"

They laughed. There was a line around the block for free gumbo.

"When things are bad in an ordinary way, we get used to it," Sammy philosophized. "Daily life is hard. We struggle and cry and complain, but we accept it. We say, 'That's the way life is.' Y'all look around today. It's not ordinary bad. It's a disaster. Yet folks only has their mind set on how to help each other. Y'all ever notice that the worst situations bring out the best?"

Jada and Ernesto listened carefully. They knew about "ordinary bad." They accepted lots of bad things as normal. Now they knew it wasn't the way it had to be.

From Sammy's Sugar Shack, they returned to Wood Street. Everywhere, people were out and about, looking for ways to help. When they reached Jada's house, they were relieved to see Alvina Russell on the porch.

"Hello, again!" she raised her hand.

"Hello, Mrs. Russell!" they cried out with relief.

"We shook and shook! We didn't fall!" she said triumphantly. "I just sent Mr. Russell a telegram to let him know we survived."

"We stopped by to make sure you weren't hurt," Misty Horn said.

"I hope your families are all right," Mrs. Russell replied.

"Earthquakes are scary," Ernesto said. "My uncle was injured in the Loma Prieta earthquake."

"Was that the big one in 1868?" Mrs. Russell asked.

"I wasn't born, but I think it was 1989. A section of the bridge collapsed, and the Cypress Freeway flattened like a pancake."

"Young man, you are confused!" Alvina said sharply.

Jada pointed towards the future Mandela Parkway. "It was over there."

"Goodness! I never heard anything about it," Mrs. Russell said.

Loaded with supplies, a dozen wagons moved slowly down Wood Street.

"I have to excuse myself," Alvina Russell apologized, picking up a pile of blankets and quilts. "They're flocking from San Francisco to Oakland wearing only their night clothes and undergarments! We can't keep them waiting or they'll freeze!"

As they turned down Seventh Street, a crowd of Chinese men, women, and children rushed towards them.

"Mr. Yuen!" Jada and Ernesto shouted.

Mr. Yuen stopped. His black jacket and pants were torn. His long hair was loose, and his *baó* askew.

"We're Johnny's friends," Jada said.

"I think Johnny is probably okay. His carriage house is made of wood. Wooden houses do well in earthquakes."

"What about you?" Jada asked, seeing a trickle of blood on his neck.

Mr. Yuen wiped his face and neck with his handkerchief. "A brick fell on me, but it's nothing serious. The Chinese are fleeing Chinatown. When bad things happen, the Chinese get blamed. Mobs are more dangerous than earthquakes. We'll be welcomed at Pacific Coast Canning Company on Pine Street. A Chinese gentleman owns it."

Misty Horn cocked his head to the west. A wind whirled around them.

"Nasty weather," Mr. Yuen said in despair.

The wind howled as Misty Horn smiled knowingly. "I think it's our time to go!"

Letter from Topaz

They recognized Chinatown from the signs and crowds and aromatic smells, but certain things had changed. In the window of a corner store was a large sign: *I AM AN AMERICAN*. In the windows of a shop on the opposite corner was another large sign: *I AM NOT JAPANESE*. What did it mean?

"Do you think we'll ever get home?" Jada asked forlornly.

"Do not fret," Misty Horn consoled her. "At least we've moved forward in time."

Ernesto stood in front of a narrow three-story building with a carved red door. "Isn't this Mr. Yuen's place?"

On the balcony sat a frail man gazing at the gray, overcast sky. He wore a blue silk shirt, khaki slacks, and sunglasses. His hair was thin and white and cut short. He had a white mustache and a wispy goatee.

"Mr. Yuen?" Ernesto called boldly.

The man's head rotated to the street. "Who's there?"

"Old friends," Ernesto said.

"All my friends are old," Mr. Yuen remarked.

"We're very old friends, but we aren't very old!" Jada laughed.

"You speak in riddles! Then you laugh!" Mr. Yuen protested. "Your riddles are hard for a blind man to solve."

"We didn't mean to be unkind," Misty Horn intervened.

"You don't sound Chinese," Mr. Yuen said.

"The last time we met was the night of the big earthquake," Jada hinted.

"So long ago? How can you still be young?"

"They're young compared to us," Misty Horn explained.

"Evil times are here again," Mr. Yuen said. "There's war all over the world."

"War up, down, and around," Misty Horn commiserated.

"Do the signs have something to do with war?" Ernesto asked.

Dorothea Lange, *Japanese Owned Grocery Store*, Oakland, March 30, 1942.

"We're afraid they look at us and think we're Japanese. Our face is our crime. Some still blame us for everything."

Ernesto understood. Immigrants were often accused of false things.

"What about the sign, *I AM AN AMERICAN?*"
Jada asked.

"My granddaughter, Li Hua, told me about that
sign. The store's owner was born in Oakland. He and
his wife and four children are U.S. citizens. Because his
parents came from Japan, the government has forced
them to close their business, leave their home, and
sell everything. They've been sent to a concentration
camp."

"Like Nazi camps?" Ernesto asked. His teacher Mr.
Nok had given him *The Diary of Anne Frank* to read.
He knew that Nazis had tortured and murdered mil-
lions, especially Jews.

"They're called internment camps, but special
words do not lessen the pain," Mr. Yuen said bitterly.
"My granddaughter is best friends with their youngest
girl. We're taking care of their dog until they return."

"Will they come back?" Ernesto wondered aloud.

Misty Horn replied softly. "Because of the camps'
poor conditions, the unhealthy food, and the terrible
emotional injury of being treated like the enemy, sadly,
some died. When they returned after the war, many
had to rebuild their lives from nothing. Others discovered their homes, businesses, farms, and fishing boats
were saved by kind neighbors. The country was angry

and frightened after the bombing of Pearl Harbor. German and Italian citizens were also affected, but no one was more persecuted than Japanese Americans. In its rush to judgment, our government made a tragic mistake. Perhaps you know what I mean?"

They knew what he meant. After 9-11, Muslim-American girls were often taunted and harassed for their *hijabs* and long dresses. Some called them "terrorists" as a joke, but it wasn't funny.

"Auntie Yates says, *If we live in fear, we can never grow and change.*"

"Auntie Yates is a wise soul," Misty Horn added.

"*Yéye!*" a young girl shouted to Mr. Yuen.

Standing beside them was Li Hua, Mr. Yuen's granddaughter. She was slender and petite, with rosy skin and glossy black hair styled in a pageboy. She wore a pleated skirt and navy blazer with white socks and brown-and-white saddle shoes. In one hand, she held a leash with a dog and in the other, a bag of plum candy.

"We have visitors," Mr. Yuen said.

"Hello," she said politely. "This is Bobo."

"Hi, Bobo!" Ernesto held out his fingers to the large, furry creature.

Li Hua bent down and hugged Bobo. "He's not my dog. He belongs to my best friend."

Mr. Yuen pointed to the mailbox. "The postman said you have a letter."

Li Hua pulled out an envelope. She touched the purple three-cent stamp and the postmark from Delta, Utah.

"It's from Yoko! Can I read it to you, *Yéye?*"

Mr. Yuen smiled tenderly at his granddaughter. He knew how it felt to be separated from family and friends. Long ago, he left many loved ones behind in China when he came to California or *Gam Saan.* In China, everyone believed he would get rich and send for them. He spent most of his life working as a cook in a private home. Nonetheless, he was rich with pride. Because of his hard work, his son and daughter went to college.

Li Hua slid her thumb under the envelope's flap. She pulled out a sheet of paper.

Dear Li Hua,

I am sorry I have not written! Since our life flipped upside down, it has been hard for me to write. I live in a camp called Topaz in the high desert where it's hotter than a hundred degrees in summer and colder than zero in winter. In a desert, there is no lake, no river, no ocean, no bay. It's nothing like Oakland.

The wind blows almost all the time, but it's not a nice wind. Dust and sand blow, too. If the sand and mud are too thick, we can't wear our shoes. Daddy made us getas to walk in.

We live in one room inside a barrack. My sister, brothers, parents, grandma, and I sleep on cots with straw mattresses. The only light is a bulb from the ceiling and a single window. It is crowded! Almost 8,000 of us live at Topaz.

The worst part is the barbed wire and guard towers. Whenever I see the guards with their guns, I think I am having a nightmare. It isn't a nightmare. We are in prison.

The other worst part is the bathroom. In between the barracks are toilets and a shower. There is NO privacy! Grandma is so embarrassed that she won't shower unless it's after midnight.

As for daddy, he found enough scrap wood to make us a table and chairs. He and my brothers also patched the holes in the walls and roof. Taichi says he's going to join the 442nd Regiment. Grandma doesn't want him to go. She doesn't want him to fight for the United States after they put us in this awful place.

The food is bad! Instead of rice, they give us potatoes. They give us ketchup to make soup.

The good things are school and sports. I'm on a baseball team. That's fun! Another good thing is the art we make with things we find. We call it gamen. Sometimes the blue blue sky and white white clouds make me happy. I wish you could see the sky, but you are lucky not to live here.

I miss you! I think about you every day! Please hug Bobo for me.

Your friend, Yoko

P.S. - *I wrote a* haiku.

Here in the desert
grandma makes mochi *for luck*
I sit while birds fly

As Li Hua finished the letter, tears streamed down her face. "That's a sad letter, *Yéye.*"

"Very sad," Mr. Yuen agreed. "I have news to cheer you up. Uncle Johnny is in town and coming for dinner."

"Johnny?" Jada and Ernesto chimed in unison.

"I guess you know Johnny from the 1906 earthquake, too!" Mr. Yuen joked.

"Do you mean Johnny as in Joãozinho?" Jada asked.

"We only call him Johnny."

"Did he like to take out your boat?" Ernesto prompted.

"When he was a boy, he pestered me every day about my sampan."

"We know Johnny!" Jada cried.

"He and I boxed once," Ernesto said.

"You must be pretty good. Johnny was a feather-weight champion."

"We're glad he escaped the mill," Misty Horn said.

"Do you know what Johnny bought with his prize money?" Mr. Yuen asked.

"A house!" Jada guessed.

"A car!" Ernesto said.

"He bought a boat and sailed around the world. His boat was his house and car."

"Hello!" A deep voice bellowed from a block away.

They pivoted to see a small, muscular man sprinting along the sidewalk. His salt-and-pepper hair was short. Thick eyebrows highlighted his tan, sun-weathered cheeks. He was dapper in gabardine slacks, a V-neck sweater, an oxford cloth shirt, a tie, a loose casual jacket, and a fedora.

Li Hua ran and jumped into his arms. "Uncle Johnny!"

"Sugar plum!" He hugged her affectionately and patted Bobo's head.

"You're staying for dinner," Li Hua commanded.

"How can I refuse? Grandpa Yuen is the best cook in Oakland!"

"You're too old to call me grandpa!" Mr. Yuen retorted. "Did you meet my other old friends?"

Johnny turned to Misty Horn. "You have a familiar face, sir."

"We've probably seen each other around the town," Misty Horn said.

"I have the impression we've conversed," Johnny insisted.

"The boy says he once boxed with you," Mr. Yuen said.

"What's with you kids!" Johnny grinned, flashing two gold teeth where there used to be holes.

"They are rascals," Mr. Yuen said. "They told me we met during the big quake."

"They're pulling your leg! They're barely older than Li Hua."

"I asked them not to torment a blind man, but I'm inviting them for dinner, too."

Johnny held up a paper bag full of *couves*. "From my sister's garden."

"We thank you, Mr. Yuen and Mr. Johnny," Misty Horn said hastily. "I'm afraid we have other plans."

CHAPTER

Double-V Blues

Oakland buzzed with life. Soldiers, sailors, and civilians flocked to restaurants, nightclubs, ballrooms, movie palaces, and department stores. After the desperate years of the Great Depression, people finally had money to spend.

Before the war, Oakland was already a vital transport hub. The city's thriving automobile industry inspired the name "Detroit of the West." The Oakland airport was one of the West Coast's most important aviation centers. The earliest pioneers of trans-Pacific flights left from Oakland, and the fortunate pilots who survived returned to Oakland, too.

Broadway was jammed with women in work clothes, holding lunch pails and satchels of gear like safety goggles and gloves. They resembled the posters of "Rosie the Riveter" pictured in her blue shirt with her hair tied up in a red-and-white polka dot bandana, flexing her biceps, with the motto: **WE CAN DO IT!**

"I guess women won more than the vote!" Ernesto said.

"Indeed! During World War II, six million women took all kinds of jobs, including welders, riveters, teamsters, painters, electricians, and tank cleaners. However, it was men who had to make the adjustment. It wasn't easy for them to work alongside women or Negroes. Women won the respect and admiration of the entire nation, but despite Executive Order 8802, we Negroes had a longer, harder road."

Misty Horn continued, "Thousands poured in from around the country to fill the jobs at factories, military bases, and shipyards. It was called the 'Second Gold Rush.' Moore Dry Dock Company at the foot of Adeline Street was the biggest shipyard in Oakland. Kaiser in Richmond was the biggest shipyard in the U.S. with 90,000 workers. Some of them commuted from West Oakland to Richmond on the 'Shipyard Railway.' Kaiser not only provided jobs and transportation but also health clinics and child care."

"Sounds pretty good," Jada said. Most of her mother's family migrated to the Bay Area from Texas and Alabama during World War II.

"Like everything, it's complicated. Millions of white men had been recruited to fight in the war so companies were forced to hire women, blacks, Mexicans, and Chinese. At first, they gave us the dumbest, most menial work: cleaning, sweeping, washing up. That was disappointing. We African Americans who came from the Deep South expected to find our California 'Promised Land.' Things here were better. Wages were considerably higher, but we were ushered to the 'colored' section of the movie theater. We couldn't patronize many hotels and ballrooms. The California Hotel on San Pablo Avenue was an exception. It was *our* place!

"Southern Negroes like me arrived in homemade clothes, with funny accents, rural manners, and high expectations about our rights. *Braceros* from Mexico and Okies from the Dust Bowl arrived with high expectations, too. Thousands of black newcomers didn't fit into the established communities of educated, professional Negroes who had lived in West Oakland for decades.

"Housing projects were quickly built to accommodate war workers and their families. Homeowners rented out extra rooms. Sometimes three men working three different shifts rented the same bed. These were nicknamed 'hot beds' because the sheets were always warm. Those who couldn't find a bed slept in one of Oakland's many movie theaters."

Misty Horn pointed to a picket line of well-dressed women and men, both African American and white.

"That's what I'm talking about!" he cried.

The picketers held up signs asking shoppers to boycott stores that refused to hire blacks.

> ## DON'T SHOP WHERE YOU CAN'T WORK!

"You understand about boycotts?" Misty Horn asked.

"We understand," Jada said. "A doctor came to our school asking us to boycott soda."

"You kids hold the power!"

"But who wants to give up soda even if it makes us sick?"

They walked through West Oakland, past the elegant Sixteenth Street railroad station. It overflowed with travelers from near and far. Families carried boxes, bundles, babies, and battered suitcases, eager to start a new life.

Everywhere they saw posters for the Double-V campaign: an eagle perched on a sun with *DOUBLE VIC-*

TORY written in the arc of the rays. Two Vs spanned the sun and eagle.

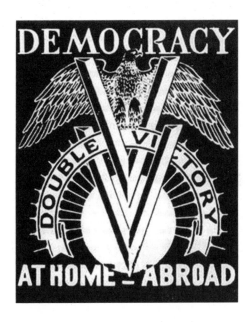

"Two enemies? Two oceans? Two Vs?" Ernesto puzzled.

"One V symbolized victory over enemies abroad like Hitler and fascism. The other V was victory over the Negroes' enemies at home, such as discrimination. Remember those 'restrictive covenants' in 1906? They still existed. There were spoken *and* unspoken rules. Even the military was segregated."

"In our time, we pretend it all went away," Jada said. "But it didn't."

"It didn't," Ernesto echoed.

In almost every window hung a blue or gold star. Blue meant your son was serving in the war. Gold meant your son had died.

"An estimated fifty million people worldwide perished in World War II," Misty Horn said.

"Astronomical," Jada said, thinking of the stars in the sky.

At school, she once saw a film about students who collected over six million paper clips to signify those slaughtered in the Nazi concentration camps. The paper clips filled a train car.

"Will your generation end the scourge of war?" Misty Horn asked them.

"We'll have to start in Oakland," Ernesto said.

"Peace inside, peace outside." Misty Horn tapped his heart.

"Double-V," Ernesto smiled wistfully.

"What about these gardens?" Jada asked, admiring the flourishing rows of vegetables that grew between houses, beside factories and stores, next to sidewalks and streets. "They're everywhere."

"These are Victory gardens," Misty Horn said. "There's a shortage of food because of the war. Folks have gone back to growing their own vegetables. Of course, blacks from the South never stopped raising our own food. Now everyone is doing their part, big and small."

Tacked to the door of the bowling alley, they read:

> **DOUBLE-V BENEFIT CONCERT**
> ***TOMMY LEE YATES***
> **SLIM JENKINS SUPPER CLUB**
> **1748 SEVENTH STREET * WEST OAKLAND**
> **TONIGHT! 9 pm!**

"Tommy Lee Yates!" Jada shouted. "Is that who I think it is?"

"He was my friend," Misty Horn said. "He could work all day in the shipyards and play music all night! That was before he married your great-grandmother, Auntie Yates."

Jada studied the photograph of the handsome young man with a guitar. "He died a long time before I was born," she said sadly.

"Can we go hear him?" Ernesto asked.

"You better believe it!" Misty Horn said.

Clubs, pool halls, card rooms, record shops, recording studios, rooming houses, hotels, barber shops, shoeshine parlors, the Lincoln Theater, corner stores, and restaurants, including a Mexican music store and Spanish-speaking movie theater, lined blocks of Seventh Street. It was music central, competing with San Francisco's Fillmore district as "Harlem of the West." Some clubs were small, with a few tables. Others were deluxe, with doormen and a lineup of famous entertainers.

Men in spiffy U.S. Army and Navy uniforms and civilians in stylish clothes, sharp shoes and hats, evening gowns, tuxedos, and zoot suits streamed into Slim Jenkins's swanky club at the corner of Wood Street. Standing by the door, a glamorous hostess welcomed the club's patrons.

"They won't let us in," Jada predicted.

"They'll let us in," Misty Horn said, digging out a tie and a Double-V membership card from his pocket.

The hostess's eyebrows rose at the sight of Jada's dirty shirt and Ernesto's low-hanging pants. "He can't come in without a jacket and tie," she said.

"I'm afraid we've been traveling," Misty Horn apologized. "I don't have an extra tie with me."

She reached in a drawer and handed Ernesto a short striped tie. She pointed to the checkroom. "He can find a jacket there. As for the young lady, she could have washed up. This is a classy club."

"Like I said, we're unprepared," Misty Horn said, flashing his Double-V card.

The hostess shrugged. It was wartime. The world had turned upside down.

"Welcome then," she said, attaching Double-V pins to their collars.

"Hey, clown!" Jada chortled at Ernesto's white dinner jacket.

"Clown yourself!" he frowned.

They passed into a mirrored bar where stools, tables, and booths were crowded with people chatting and laughing.

Jada clapped to the jazzy tune on the jukebox. "I've never seen anything like this!"

"Back in the day, nightclubs and dance halls were popular entertainment. Since blacks usually couldn't go to white clubs, they created their own."

"Whites are here," Ernesto noted.

"When it comes to music, whites always do like the *colored*!" Misty Horn said.

"Cool!" Ernesto cried.

Jada thumped him on the head. "You've got to expand your vocabulary!"

They followed another hostess to the dining room and a table covered in a white tablecloth. A waitress set out linen napkins, silverware, and menus.

"What do you recommend?" Misty Horn asked, glancing at the choices.

"Not much," the waitress said. "We haven't gotten fresh meat in a week. We ran out of sugar two days ago. The government docked the Italian-owned boats so we rarely have fish. The milk delivery didn't come today."

Ernesto read the menu.

T-BONE STEAK – 50 CENTS
CHICKEN – 25 CENTS
HAM AND EGGS – 35 CENTS

"No meat, sugar, milk, or fish," he repeated.

"We've got ration cards like everybody else," she complained. "Anyway where are y'all from? It looks like y'all have been on the road for days."

"West Oakland," Jada piped up.

The hostess regarded her suspiciously. "Frankly, I'm in no mood for jokes!"

"The kids are tired and confused," Misty Horn said. "We'll be grateful if you bring us whatever is available."

As it turned out, the meal was excellent. There was bread, collard greens, bowls of spaghetti, three drumsticks, and strawberry ice cream for dessert.

"You want to dance?" Ernesto asked.

Jada laughed. "As in Aztec dancing?"

He held out his hand. "My *papá* taught me how to swing dance."

"You're crazy!" she laughed louder.

"Watch me!" Misty Horn spun on one foot and caught the hand of a pretty woman. He twirled his partner as the entire room burst into song:

He was a famous trumpet man
From old Chicago way
He had a boogie style
That no one else could play
He was the top man at his craft
But then his number came up
And he was gone with the draft
He's in the Army now
Blowin' reveille
He's the boogie-woogie bugle boy of Company B!

"Hey, pops!" the young woman said. "You still got your Lindy Hop moves!"

"I guess so," Misty Horn panted.

"Come on, Dottie!" a young woman called.

"Theresa, hold on! Let me catch my breath! Pops here wore me out!"

"Theresa?" Jada gasped, recognizing a younger version of her great-grandmother.

A statuesque woman with strong, chiseled features and a bobbed hairdo walked towards them. She was dressed in a gold lamé dress, glittering high heels, and a gold lamé beret. Her skin and hair resembled Maisha's, but her nose and mouth were like Jada's.

Misty Horn gave Jada a dire warning. "No direct conversation!" he ordered.

Theresa reprimanded Dottie. "Tommy Lee is waiting for us backstage!"

Dottie winked at Jada. "Tommy Lee this! Tommy Lee that! All day at welding school, it's Tommy Lee! You'd think they were in love!"

"They *are* in love," Jada said to herself.

Dottie pinched Jada's cheek. "Where we come from, working in a white woman's kitchen is about the only job a Negro woman can get. Here in Oakland, we are independent!"

"We want to be the first Negro women to weld the ships that win the war!" Theresa said.

"If she can take her eyes off Tommy Lee!" Dottie added.

"Hush!" Theresa scolded. "Or I'll tell them about your nutty boyfriend, Misty Horn. You *never* stop talking about him!"

Ernesto and Jada stared at each other with amazement.

"This is Misty . . . ," Ernesto stopped himself.

"We've got to go!" Theresa grabbed Dottie's hand, and they skittered over the floor.

"Is that *really* who I think it is?" Jada asked.

"It's your Auntie Yates before she married Tommy Lee. As for Dottie, she was once my girl."

Jada and Ernesto looked at Misty Horn. With his fuzzy white hair and wrinkled face, the gray circles that shadowed his eyes, and the liver spots that sprinkled his hands, it was hard to imagine him young. He was missing a tooth, his dry lips were cracked, his fingers shook, and sometimes it was difficult for him to walk. But Misty Horn could still dance, and he'd been in love with Dottie.

"Tell us," Jada pleaded.

"I don't need to tell you anything," Misty Horn said, wiping away a tear. "You can see for yourself. Life is good and bad, glad and sad, bitter and sweet."

Jada and Ernesto ruminated on his words. As young as they were, they knew what he said was true.

At nine o'clock, Theresa Lyle stepped up to the microphone. "Good evening," she greeted the roomful of patrons.

Ernesto poked Jada. "Auntie Yates! Can you believe it?"

"Hush!" Jada said.

"We are gathered tonight for a very special reason. While we continue to fight for democracy in Europe and across the Pacific, we cannot forget the vigilant fight we have here at home."

The crowd broke into applause.

"Let me quote from James G. Thompson's letter:

The 'V for Victory' sign is being displayed prominently in all so-called democratic countries which are fighting for victory over aggression, slavery and tyranny. If this V sign means that to those now engaged in this great conflict, then let colored Americans adopt the double VV for a double victory."

Everyone clapped loudly again.

"Double-V is the newest campaign for Negro equality. I hope you'll wear your Double-V pins. Hang your Double-V banners on your doors. Join a Double-V club. Consider making a donation and join us next week to hear Elmer Keeton's Bay Area Negro Chorus."

Theresa Lyle threw her hands in the air and made the V-sign. The audience threw their hands in the air and made the V-sign, too.

"It is my great pleasure to introduce Tommy Lee Yates, a man who needs no introduction."

The applause was thunderous.

A man stepped shyly onto the stage. He tipped his hat and loosened his tie. He tuned his guitar and took a finger pick and bottleneck from his pocket. Then he hugged Theresa Lyle and whispered in her ear, "Thank you, sweetheart."

The microphone reverberated through the room. *Thank you, sweetheart! Thank you, sweetheart! Thank you, sweetheart!*

Tommy Lee reddened with embarrassment as everybody roared with laughter. Without a word, he began to play a string of songs brought to Oakland from the work fields of the South and tough streets of the North, a special sound that created West Coast blues.

Listeners laughed and cried as the music described the essence of life: *good, bad, glad, sad, bitter, sweet.*

On the last note of Tommy Lee's final song, Misty Horn rose from the table.

"We better go before Jada starts yammering to her great-grandmother," he said.

"What about Tommy Lee's autograph?" she begged.

"Jada Yates, has anyone ever called you a pest?" Misty Horn teased.

After Ernesto deposited his jacket and tie at the checkroom, he and Jada waited outside the club. The smells of low tide and creosote from the ships filled the air. In fact, it was very dark. As a precaution against enemy attacks, blackout curtains covered every window. Fear of attack was so great that an antisubmarine net had been stretched across part of San Francisco Bay.

Nevertheless, the atmosphere was festive. In fact, the dangers, fears, and anxieties of war gave people the bond of common cause. They enjoyed themselves because life itself was precious and short.

Misty Horn reappeared with a menu from Slim Jenkins. Scribbled on it, Jada read:

Follow your star—
Tommy Lee Yates, Blues Man

Gusts of wind whistled over the roofs and treetops. Crowds and clubs disappeared in a thick vapor of fog. Mist swirled around their heads. They shivered in the chilly air, held hands, and closed their eyes as they said:

The harder we look, the more we see!
The more we stare, the sooner we get there!

All Power to All the People

A dozen children were seated on a carpet, their legs folded, their hands held loosely in their laps, and their eyes closed. In front of them sat a young woman with a big Afro and silver hoop earrings, wearing bell-bottom jeans and a black leather jacket. Her eyes were closed too, her arms extended, and her middle fingers and thumbs touching.

"Notice where your body makes contact with the floor: your bottom, your legs, your ankles," she said softly. "Feel your feet in your socks, your arms in your sleeves, the air on your face and hands. As you inhale and exhale, notice your breath. Don't change your breath. Just notice the sensations inside your nose and movement of your lungs. As you inhale, picture a light entering the bottom of your spine and rising through the crown of your head, shining positive energy throughout your body and mind."

Ernesto and Jada watched with fascination.

As the woman spoke, the children's bodies relaxed. Their mouths didn't smile, but it was as if their whole bodies were smiling on the inside. When they opened their eyes, they were startled to see Jada and Ernesto.

"I've been waiting for you!" the young woman with the Afro greeted them.

"Us?" Jada asked.

"Absolutely," she laughed with ease. "I need help with breakfast!"

"Aren't they fed at school?" Jada asked.

"This *is* school. Not a public school! They barely get pencils and books there. They certainly don't get food. At this school, they get breakfast, lunch, *and* dinner. Years before *Brown v. Board of Education*, California beat segregation with *Mendez v. Westminster.* In reality, segregation still beats us. That's why *we* are here."

"*We* who?" Ernesto asked.

"The Black Panthers!"

"BLL-ACK PANN-THERSSS! For real!"

The young woman's voice grew serious. "What's real are hungry kids, lead poisoning, elders stuck at home, schools without working toilets or heat!" Her eyes widened. "If you're new to Oakland, I better clue you in. Crime is about the best career choice for our young people. As for city services, forget it. There aren't piddling dollars to fix anything. The government's solution is 'Tear It Down'! I guess they think we'll disappear, too. They call it *urban renewal!* They think it's catchy, but we're not fooled! They ripped through our communities to build freeways. Now they're tearing them up again to build BART. That's real!"

"We know what happened to Seventh Street in West Oakland," Jada said.

"We also know about kids and jobs," Ernesto said. "A long time ago, we had a friend who worked in a cotton mill in Jingletown. He was barely thirteen."

"It couldn't be so long ago, brother!" she declared. "You're not old yourselves. As for Jingletown, the Nimitz Freeway split it in half like the freeways chopped up West Oakland. Soon nobody will remember what used to be. They'll think freeways were always here. A fact of life like something natural."

"We don't believe that!" Jada protested.

"They build the things on landfill in poor neighborhoods," Ruthie said. "Nobody pays attention until an earthquake shakes them loose."

"That'll happen," Ernesto said.

"Listen to the young prophet! I won't be surprised if it all falls down!"

"We've heard of Huey Newton and Bobby Seale," Jada said.

"I guess so! They're famous all over the world. The more I learn, the more I realize leaders do not make a movement. It takes all of us, including you two." She grasped their arms. "James Baldwin says, 'Millions of anonymous people is what history is about.'"

"Cool," Ernesto said.

"Hey, my name is Ruthie Singleton! All power to all the people!" Her face brightened. "What are the names of my save-the-day helpers?"

"I'm Jada Yates. This is Ernesto Cruz." Jada turned towards the door. "And Misty . . . "

Misty Horn was slumped on the steps.

"Do what the sister asks," he waved. "I'll be along in a minute."

"Jada and Ernesto, you are Tuesday's miracle!"

Ruthie led them to the kitchen. Cartons of eggs, loaves of whole wheat bread, turkey sausage, and orange juice were on the counter. Ernesto glanced at the large, boxy radio on the shelf.

"Sounds like Tommy Lee Yates," he said.

Ruthie checked the radio dial. "For great music and what's really going down, we listen to KDIA or KPFA. Are you a Lucky 13 fan?"

"I don't have a radio," Ernesto said.

"No radio! How do you live?"

"I've got a . . . ," Ernesto stopped to think of a word. "It's a gizmo."

"Gizmo, huh? Well, whatever works. We better get the eggs scrambled."

"I can scramble eggs," Jada said. "I can make bread from scratch, too."

"Let me cook the eggs," Ernesto said. "I work at a *taquería* in East Oakland."

"Sister, can you keep the children entertained?" Ruthie asked.

Jada smiled. Instead of "colored," she was "sister." Things had definitely improved!

"Y'all like to sing?" she asked the kids.

A group of young brown, black, white, and Asian kids all wagged their heads. At the Oakland Community School, they sang at every assembly.

Jada searched her brain. No rap, no way. "Do you have a favorite song?" she asked.

A girl, no older than six, opened her mouth. A song bellowed through the room into the hall and out to the street.

We can make this world like it should be,
We can do anything, you and me!

Jada listened as the other children joined. While some sang, others formed a circle and danced. Jada had never seen children behave so freely, so sure of themselves.

Ruthie and Ernesto appeared, balancing trays of scrambled eggs and toast.

"You do this every day?" Jada asked.

"This and more! The Panthers run free breakfast sites for kids and a free health clinic in South Berkeley. Those are two of our 'survival programs,'" Ruthie said. "This is our free elementary school on East Fourteenth Street. On weekends, the school turns into a community center. Other groups meet here, like the Brown Berets. You know about them?"

"Are they a gang?" Ernesto asked.

"You're fooling with me!" Ruthie winked.

Sometimes the faces of his old gang flickered in Ernesto's mind. Two or three had been like brothers. The others, he should never have trusted.

We can make this world like it should be.

"It's hard to change the world on an empty stomach or empty mind," Ruthie said. "If we can cover basic needs, people will have time and energy to work for change."

"We helped out after an earthquake," Jada said proudly. "That's where we learned to make bread. It wasn't charity. It was called 'mutual aid.'"

"It's always good to help out," Ruthie said. "Then you can understand what it means to survive man-made disasters on a daily basis. We call our disaster 'slow violence' because it takes its toll over many years and many generations. It's so slow powerful folks can look the other way and pretend the problems can't be fixed. Or claim it's *our* fault. As long as there are more people than decent jobs, folks will work for low wages. That perpetuates the cycle of poverty."

"It must cost lots of money to feed kids and run a free school," Jada said.

"You tell me who gets rich off the people's misery?"

"Like drug dealers?"

"Right on!" Ruthie said. "The drug dealers on the street are the small fry. They take most of the risk for the least money. The big shots take the least risk and make the most money. It's a food chain, right? However, we're on the street, too, offering an alternative. When we started the first breakfast program, we asked West Oakland's liquor barons to pay for it. They threw us a few token dollars. They got great publicity about their efforts to *help* the community, but the program needed long-term support, not tokens. Besides talking the talk, we are walking the walk with other survival programs: educating and screening for sickle cell anemia, services for our elders, food giveaways, adult education classes, teen programs, legal aid, on and on."

Ernesto and Jada regarded Ruthie with total admiration.

"If you visit our classrooms, you might be surprised. Students are grouped by ability and interests, not age. Our teaching philosophy emphasizes *how* to think, not *what* to think. If there's a problem, kids meet with a council of their peers to help work it out."

"They look happy," Jada said.

"They're loved," Ruthie said.

After breakfast, Ernesto and Jada helped clean up.

Ruthie suggested, "Later we can go to our free store to find y'all some shoes."

"Moms paid a bundle for my shoes!" Jada said.

"You got robbed! What about your pants, young brother?"

"It's the style," Ernesto admitted.

"We can find you a belt at the free store, too. As for our beautiful sister."

"Me?" Jada asked.

Ruthie rummaged in her purse and pulled out two T-shirts. "This is a thank-you gift for helping me," she said.

Jada slipped on the *BLACK IS BEAUTIFUL* shirt.

"You look like a queen!" Ruthie exclaimed.

Jada smiled. She felt proud *and* black *and* beautiful.

"Hey, do y'all live nearby?" Ruthie asked.

"Deep East," Ernesto said, pulling the *POWER TO THE PEOPLE* T-shirt over his head.

"When I was a little girl, my auntie had a house in Elmhurst. On Sundays, we often went to the Oakland Airport. In those days, the airport was big entertainment. We watched the planes take off and land. We never got tired of it. You live at Tassa?"

"Tassa is way different now," Ernesto said. "It's a *green* building. The old Tassa was a crime magnet. They tore it down."

"Tore it down? They just built it! Anyway Tassa looks better than the projects in West Oakland."

"Maybe it was nice in the 1960s," Ernesto said.

"Last time I checked, this is the '60s!" Ruthie spun around. "I hope you're not hooked on funny weed."

"It's a vision thing I have," Ernesto said. "Like someday there will be beautiful housing for everyone and native plants on the roof for birds to nest."

"Let's make that vision come true!" Ruthie said.

Jada reached for her abalone pendant. "I wish you could see an Ohlone village," she said.

Ernesto stuffed the pendant back into Jada's pocket. "She has visions, too!"

"Maybe you'll become storytellers," Ruthie said. "Words are our most powerful tool for change."

"I want to be an astronomer," Jada said.

"That's a big dream!" Ruthie said.

"Have you heard of Benjamin Banneker and his *Almanac* in the 1700s or Maria Mitchell in the 1800s or Beth Brown or Mae Jemison?" Jada asked.

"You already know a lot," Ruthie beamed. "If you need to save for college, lots of young people sell our newspaper, *The Black Panther*."

"We probably can't stay long," Ernesto said.

"It's almost time for us to go," Jada confirmed.

"Can I ask you to remember one thing? Change isn't only possible, it's inevitable! The time for People Power is now! By the way, let me give you a copy of our reading list. Then you can understand what's going down on the streets here and in Vietnam."

"Like Double-V!" Ernesto raised his thumb.

"Like *Speaking Truth to Power!*" Ruthie raised her fist. "Our Ten-Point Program asks you to be part of something bigger than yourself. You ever dream that dream?"

Jada and Ernesto nodded. They had dreamed it lots of different ways.

"It's true we have enemies in high places," Ruthie said.

Jada already knew some of the reasons that things fell apart. "My Auntie Patricia worked at the Black Panthers' Free Health Clinic," she said.

"Your auntie?" Ruthie asked. "I think I know her. She can explain what went down with police harassment, power plays, undercover informers, false arrests, the FBI's COINTELPRO, and assassinations. However, our school thrives, and our programs survive. We are a peoples' movement, or, as brother Fred said, 'a rainbow coalition.'"

"I like that," Ernesto said. "All the colors of the rainbow."

"Across the water, our Indian brothers and sisters are claiming Alcatraz Island. The Diggers are feeding and clothing youth in San Francisco. The Brown Berets are inspiring a Chicano movement. Asian brothers and sisters are occupying the International Hotel. East in the valleys of California, Filipinos and Mexicans are organizing farm workers. *All power to all the people!*"

"All power to all the people!" Misty Horn said feebly as he staggered into the room.

Ruthie rushed to his side. "Are you sick, brother?"

"Misty Horn!" Jada clutched his hand.

"Our time!" he croaked.

Ruthie patted his forehead. "He's delirious!"

"Can we drive him to Highland?" Ernesto asked.

"No hospital," Misty Horn moaned.

"None of the old-timers trust white doctors," Ruthie explained. "When it comes to medicine, we're accustomed to taking care of ourselves. But we're connected to white doctors and nurses who care."

"No doctor!" Misty Horn groaned.

Ruthie felt his wrist. "I can't find a pulse!" she cried. "Call the operator!"

"I don't have my cell!" Ernesto said.

Ruthie pointed to a phone mounted on the wall beside the kitchen. "Dial 0 for operator and tell them it's an emergency!"

Through the doorway, the wind began to blow. Ernesto and Jada huddled over Misty Horn.

"Maybe we're finally going home," Jada said.

OAKLAND TALES

THE PRESENT AGAIN

If stories come to you, care for them.

*And learn to give them away
where they are needed.*

*Sometimes a person needs a story
more than food to stay alive.*

{ Barry Lopez }

The Funeral

This time, there was no doubt. They were inside Jada's attic room. The lavender walls, the colorful pillows, the stuffed animals, and star map on the wall confirmed it was *their* time. Outside, a few stars twinkled, streetlights glowed, BART trains squealed, and sirens raced through West Oakland.

Misty Horn lay on Jada's bed, his eyes closed, his breathing erratic.

"We're here," Jada said.

"I'm glad," Misty Horn whispered. "I didn't want to die there."

"You're not going to die," Ernesto insisted.

"I guess I went too far too fast," Misty Horn muttered.

"You scared us," Jada said.

Sharon stood in the doorway, arms akimbo. She pointed to Misty Horn.

"We're taking him to the hospital!"

"I'm better, sister," he countered.

"You're the color of ash!" she observed. "Not a good sign for a black man!"

"He doesn't like doctors," Jada said.

"Even Auntie Yates agrees that he needs to go to Highland."

Ernesto scooped up Misty Horn and carried him down to the front door.

"When Sharon called upstairs and no one answered, we grew alarmed!" Auntie Yates said.

"We were in the attic annex," Jada explained.

"He likely had an asthma attack!" Sharon said with exasperation.

"I don't have asthma," Misty Horn said.

"If you don't have it yet, you can still get it. With all the cars, trains, ships, and diesel trucks around here, there's nothing but pollution. Have you heard of 'adult onset'? I bet that's what ails you."

Sharon drove south on 880. Although she was an excellent driver, she was nervous. She could see that Misty Horn was very sick, possibly from a heart attack.

"Moms, do you know that freeways messed up our whole community?"

"I don't need to know anything about it. I need you to put your full attention on Misty Horn. You hear what I'm saying?"

Misty Horn squeezed Jada's thumb. "Keep asking the big questions," he murmured.

Jada had never been to Highland Hospital. She didn't know how huge it was. As for Ernesto, he hated the sight of it. His friend, Freddy Sanchez, had died at Highland.

Jada and Ernesto propped Misty Horn between them and slowly walked into the emergency room. They seated him in a chair and went to check in. The admitting nurse looked up from her computer screen. Her face registered surprise, recognition, and concern.

"Ernesto, is that you?"

"Hello, Mrs. Perry! I didn't know you worked here."

"Five days a week, rain or shine," Jeannie Gray Dove Perry said, taking Ernesto's hand. "When Leonard told me you quit the gym, we got worried. We went to the *taquería*, but they hadn't seen you. Then your English teacher, Mr. Nok, tracked me down. He found an apprenticeship for you but didn't know where you were. We decided you went off to Mexico without a word."

"I couldn't tell anybody where I was," Ernesto said.

"If there was trouble, you should have come to our house," Mrs. Perry said. She scanned their soiled clothes, dirty faces, and uncombed hair. "Is one of you sick?"

Jada pointed to Misty Horn. His head drooped on Sharon's shoulder.

"My mom is afraid he had a heart attack," Jada said.

Mrs. Perry pushed a button and barked into a phone. Two orderlies arrived immediately and lifted a semi-conscious Misty Horn into a wheelchair and took him away.

"Why didn't you get me sooner?" Sharon scowled.

"He was fine," Jada said. "It was only after we got to the school . . ."

"School!" Sharon rolled her eyes. "You're telling me that three of you left the attic, walked down those creaky stairs, and out the door without my hearing you? Impossible! I hear as good as a cat!"

Jada and Ernesto were silent. Whatever they said was sure to sound crazy.

"Past ten o'clock at night and y'all talking about school!"

They sat in the waiting room, staring at the walls, the vending machines, the linoleum floor. The minutes passed slowly.

When Jada removed her jacket, Sharon's eyes rolled again.

"Why are you wearing my *BLACK IS BEAUTIFUL* T-shirt? I don't lend that shirt to anybody. It's beyond precious. Uncle Lewis gave it to me after he marched from Selma to Montgomery."

"Moms, it's not your shirt," Jada said.

"We're sorry, Mrs. Yates," Ernesto said. "We had no idea so much time had passed."

"Like hundreds of years!" Jada giggled.

"Y'all carry on with your little jokes," Sharon said. "Please, I don't want to hear any more tall tales."

When Sharon inquired about Misty Horn's condition, she was told he was stable. The next time, she was told he was undergoing tests. When Jeannie Perry's shift was over, she asked if they needed a ride.

"I can drive you anywhere," she said.

"I've got my wagon," Sharon replied. "We're going home, too."

"I just checked on Mr. Horn," Jeannie Perry said. "He's asleep."

"Mrs. Perry, I'll take a ride," Ernesto said.

"Aren't you coming with us?" Sharon protested.

"I need to see Tía Nina," he said.

"Is that okay?" Jada asked anxiously.

"Things have probably cooled off," Ernesto assured her.

"It hasn't been very long," Jada said.

"It feels like forever!"

Jeannie Perry suggested that Ernesto spend the night at their house. "That way, I know where you are," she said.

In the morning, she fixed *huevos rancheros*, black beans, fry bread, and *chile verde*.

"It's as good as breakfast at the Peraltas' *fandango*!" Ernesto said.

"What *fandango*?" she scolded. "Did you run off to go dancing?"

Ernesto smiled sheepishly. "Something like that!"

Mrs. Perry drove Ernesto to Tía Nina's house. Tía Nina was in her backyard in her straw sunbonnet and padded gloves. Nearby was a basket of her garden tools.

"*¡Hola!*" Ernesto shouted.

She wheeled around. Shock passed over her face. "You've come back already?"

"Aren't you happy to see me?" Ernesto asked.

"I am always happy to see you, *mi corazón*, but today is a bad day. It's Paco's funeral."

"No!" Ernesto cried.

"*¡Es verdad!*"

Ernesto sunk to the ground, his head in his hands.

"Is Paco dead? That's not possible!"

"You should stay over there," Tía Nina said.

Ernesto lifted his tear-stained face. "Where's the funeral?

"*No sé,*" she said.

"*¡Dime!*"

"Only if you promise not to go."

"I have to say good-bye to Paco."

Paco was his oldest friend. Paco was like a true brother. Paco never wanted to harm anyone. His sweetness made it hard for him to say no. What should have been his strength was turned into a weakness. The older boys took advantage of his sweet disposition. They asked him to do things he shouldn't do. That's how Paco got in trouble.

"*Ven aquí,*" Tía Nina said.

Ernesto followed Tía Nina to the side garden. Orange marigold petals lay scattered between the house and fence. On top of a flat rock was a piece of smoldering resin or *copal,* a chocolate bar, a stuffed bear, two white candles, and a bouquet of red poppies.

"I made the *ofrenda* for Paco," she said. "I made it to help him find peace."

Ernesto inhaled the incense. He watched the candle flames dance in the wind. He touched the ruffled edges of the poppies. A sob caught in his throat.

Tía Nina rested her hand on his head. "Today, you say *adiós* to Paco in your heart. It's no longer about Paco. Paco is gone. Your future is waiting for you."

CHAPTER 27

Tassa

Ernesto heeded Tía Nina's advice. He didn't go to the funeral. Or try to find a ride to the cemetery. He sat in the house, thinking of the past. The distant past and near past revolved in his mind. He had learned so much, but there was something missing. It was something important that he needed to understand.

Late in the afternoon after Tía Nina went out, Ernesto changed his clothes. He dressed in drab colors. He put on dark green and navy. He combed his hair a different way. He turned up the collar of his jacket. He went out and walked underneath the BART tracks towards the gym.

As he walked, he thought of Paco. He asked himself what he could have done. An image of the bear and bull appeared. He heard the roar of the spectators. He tasted the dust and smelled the sweat of the horses. He approached the animals as if he weren't afraid of anything. Back in East Oakland, he was afraid.

He stopped at the entrance to Tassafaronga. He admired the new buildings, large windows, the walkways, and gardens of native plants. Children bounded over the grass, laughing and playing games. They were all sizes, all colors, shouting in different languages. Nearby their families chatted and cooked on outdoor grills.

"Hey, young man! Are you hungry?" a stranger called out. In his hand were tongs and a piece of chicken.

A woman smiled. "You like *markouk*?" she asked in a heavy accent. "I made too much."

"No, thanks," Ernesto said. He didn't have time. He was already late to meet Leonard at the boxing gym.

He left the perimeter of Tassafaronga and entered the street. A few feet away, a young woman in a long dress and *hijab* bent forward to smell a flower. At the same instant, a car rounded the corner and screeched to a stop in front of Ernesto. In front were Hector Lobo and José Santiago. In back was Paco's brother, Franco Flores.

Ernesto's chest boiled with anger. The gang had sent Paco into danger, and now Paco was dead. Then he heard his coach's voice. *You walk away. That's how a wise man handles trouble.*

"Ernesto and Paco were like brothers," Franco said.

Hector spit at Ernesto's feet. "We know all about it," he said.

When Ernesto looked into Hector's eyes, he saw two dark holes. Whatever had been soft and loving was gone. Drilled away. Ernesto looked at José Santiago's eyes. His holes were jumpy and confused. The desperate, brittle glaze in Franco's eyes made it seem as if he didn't care what happened to himself or anyone else.

José's arm stretched through the car window. At the end of it, his stubby fingers gripped a gun. Ernesto heard the trigger cock and release. His eardrums stung with the explosion. Then the car raced away, lurching crazily from one side of the street to the other.

Ernesto felt himself melt in slow motion to the sidewalk. Voices passed through his mind, the same voices from his nightmare. His mother, *Te amo, hijo.* His coach, *That's how a wise man handles trouble.* His teacher, *You can do anything you put your mind to.* With the voices was a collage of pictures: Ohlone dancers, the Peraltas' *ramada*, Johnny and the sampan, Mr. Yuen and his granddaughter, *I AM AN AMERICAN*, Tommy Lee and his guitar, *WELCOME FRIENDS &*

STRANGERS, and sister Ruthie Singleton. He wished he could go back. Backwards in time, anywhere but here. Here his life meant *nada*. Here he was worthless. Here he was dead. Red spots filled his eyes. Sun, sky, street vanished.

He felt the presence of someone. He recoiled. *Was it enemy or friend? Reality or hallucination? Death or dream?*

His eyelids fluttered. He stared into two deep golden-brown eyes, the same color as his mother's and the shape of almonds. *Not his mother*, he thought. His mother's eyes were tired and weary. These eyes were clear. He blinked at the shining eyes and purple flower.

"Someone is coming," the gentle voice said.

Enemy or friend? Reality or hallucination? Death or dream?

She knew that she should run to get help, but she was scared to leave him.

"Don't die," she said, bending down to the ground. "If you promise not to die, I'll tell you a story."

Ernesto's eyelids fluttered again. With her flowing scarf and long dress, the young woman resembled an illustration of Scheherazade, the heroine in the book *Arabian Nights*. Scheherazade saved herself from death by telling fabulous stories to a vengeful king. Her exciting stories were long and complicated, too long to finish in one night. In the morning, the king still wanted to hear the story so he always spared her life for one more day. This went on for one thousand and one nights. Ernesto had read *Arabian Nights*. He knew about Scheherazade's cleverness, courage, and strength.

"When I was small, I came to Oakland from Syria with my family," she began.

Ernesto's head wobbled. His lips moved but made no sound. He tried to listen, but he was thirsty. He was thirstier than he had ever been. His tongue was swollen and his mouth full of sand. Maybe he wasn't in Oakland. Maybe he was in the Sonoran Desert. Maybe he had fainted from the blast of heat. But he wasn't hot. He was icy cold. He shivered and shook with chills.

She laid a sweater on his chest. As long as he could hear, he wasn't dead.

"It's a beautiful place, Syria." Her words flowed over him like a warm stream. "The sea, sand, birds, buildings, and people. Most of all, the people are beautiful. My parents built a house near the sea. They built it stone by stone, brick by brick. Until then, I thought I would write and tell stories."

"Like Scheherazade?" Ernesto tried to speak, but pain gripped every part of him.

"I began to build, too," she laughed. "I made buildings with cassette boxes. I turned them into towers. I painted the edges to look like buildings in Damascus." She wiped her eyes. So many buildings in her country had been destroyed by war. "Now I no longer wanted to be a writer but a builder. Brick by brick, I wanted to make the world beautiful." Her laughter tinkled like bells.

"I hear you," he wanted to say.

"When we came to Oakland, we didn't go outside. If we weren't at school, we stayed indoors. Our neighbors were like us. They had also fled war, poverty, and persecution. They came from Sudan, Guatemala, Vietnam, Iraq. The apartments were crowded. The bathrooms had broken sinks and toilets. The kitchens were infested with bugs. The landlord refused to fix anything. We had to pay for repairs. There was no place to study or read. Then we had a chance to move here. It's different now that we live in a beautiful place."

This is what I need to understand, Ernesto thought. *This is what I need to understand.*

The Closest Star

It was hard for Jada to sleep. She tossed and turned with worry over Misty Horn. Her mind raced from one thing to another. If they'd returned before World War II, maybe he wouldn't have gotten sick. Maybe the crazy dancing wore him out or seeing Dottie was too much of a shock.

In the kitchen, she found a note from her mother:

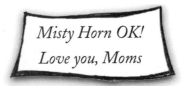

Misty Horn OK!
Love you, Moms

That was a great relief, but she still worried. Most of all, she needed to talk to Ernesto before the magical moments of the past slipped away. She needed his reassurance that their journey wasn't a game or trick or illusion.

Underneath her pile of dirty clothes, Jada reached into the pocket of her cargo pants. It was still there. She touched it. She turned it over. She felt its smooth rim. She tilted it in the sunlight to see its iridescent colors shimmer. She found a thin velvet ribbon in her jewelry box and attached the abalone pendant around her neck.

She searched her other pockets. There were acorns from the *rancho*, a shell from Goat Island, a mushy piece of plum candy from Li Hua. Next to her shoes and socks lay the *BLACK IS BEAUTIFUL* T-shirt. She pinched herself. Yes, they were real.

She still needed to speak to Ernesto. She dialed Tía Nina's number. It rang and rang. She tried the number again. No answer. That bothered her. Tía Nina liked to stay home. Ernesto wasn't supposed to leave the house.

Jada made her bed. She straightened her room. She washed her clothes and hung them on the line to dry. She dialed Tía Nina's house again and again.

Where were they? she wondered.

"Hello!" she cried when the phone rang.

"We just heard about Misty Horn," Maisha cried.

"He's better," Jada said.

"Did he get sick while you were *away?*" Maisha asked.

"*Away?*" Jada asked in turn.

"Didn't you guess that I'd gone traveling with Misty Horn, too?"

"We have a lot to discuss," Jada said.

"I know, but I called to see if you can go with us to visit him at the hospital."

"I have Champions of Science this afternoon. We're going to Chabot for the first time with our teacher," Jada said.

"Misty Horn wouldn't want you to miss that!" Maisha said.

At two o'clock, Jada walked to her school. She and the other selected students from West Oakland waited for Mrs. Grant and her minivan. They rode south on 580 to Lincoln Avenue, crossed Highway 13 to Skyline Boulevard, and drove up into the Oakland hills.

"You're going to love this program," Mrs. Grant said.

A ripple of excitement passed through them as they recognized the domes with the planetarium and telescopes. They all had questions about outer space. Here they would find answers.

"Can we look through a telescope?" a boy asked.

"On Friday and Saturday nights, the telescopes are free and open to the public if the weather is clear. However, we can see one star without a telescope." Mrs. Grant gazed up at the sky. "If you multiply the size of the earth a million times, that's the size of the sun. It's hard to imagine such a big number."

Jada thought about the millions of paper clips in a railroad car in Tennessee. Millions, billions, trillions, the infinite universe reached beyond numbers.

"Has anyone been here?" Mrs. Grant asked her students.

They shook their heads.

"Jada, you seem to hesitate."

"I was here before Chabot was built," she admitted.

"Before? You weren't even born!" Mrs. Grant said. Sometimes her students had too much imagination.

"I can show you the Navigation Trees," Jada offered.

"Jada Yates, you are teasing! There are no trees, only a plaque."

"Can we see the plaque?" a girl asked.

"Let's ask Jada why these trees were important long ago."

Memory of the great trees filled Jada with sadness and awe. "They were hundreds of feet tall, tens of feet around, as old as two thousand years, and one of the largest living things on the planet," she said. "Ships sailing into San Francisco Bay used them as guides to navigate around the danger of Blossom Rock."

"That's an excellent summary," Mrs. Grant nodded her approval.

Jada liked knowing things, but information wasn't enough. Information was merely the beginning of understanding. "The trees were important for other reasons, too," she said hesitantly.

"Was there something you wanted to add?" Mrs. Grant asked.

Jada was nervous as she spoke. "The height, the circumference, the age, the ships, those aren't the most important reasons that we remember the Navigation Trees. What's important is that they provided balance for the land and watershed. They helped to sustain the forest for thousands of years. As more people moved here, what did they see? Trees were things to cut down and sell. If the trees were here today, they'd have much to teach us." Jada blushed with embarrassment. "Sorry, I got carried away."

"You're a deep thinker," Mrs. Grant said. "Never apologize for that."

They followed their teacher into the building. They met Robin Muñoz. Robin was a junior at Fremont High School. She explained the Champions of Science program: hands-on experiments, films, and hikes in the forest. She showed them exhibits, classrooms, and labs.

"Everyone is here because they love what you love," Robin told them. "When you get older, you can become a Galaxy Explorer like me and teach visitors how to work the telescopes. You won't believe what's out there in our universe!"

Bad News Travels Fast

"Where have you been?" Sharon yelled.

Jada glared at her mother. "Moms, I told you last night. Mrs. Grant took us to Chabot today."

"I forgot," Sharon cried. "I came home and didn't find you."

"Moms, you can't be scared all the time. Remember what Auntie Yates says? *If we live in fear, we can't grow and change.*"

Sharon pulled Jada into her arms and cradled her. "My young Champion of Science, I'm so proud of you!"

"Moms, it's beautiful up there. It's a real forest."

Sharon smiled sadly. "After I heard the bad news, I forgot about everything else!"

"What? What?" Jada tugged her mother's hand. "Did something happen to Misty Horn?"

"Misty is fine, but . . . "

"Are you sick? Did Auntie Yates fall down? Is Auntie Patricia in the hospital? Tell me!"

Sharon studied Jada. Jada had changed. When she sat, she didn't slouch. When she walked, she held her head high. When she looked, her gaze was open and trusting. Most of all, she showed that she cared about others.

"Tell me, Moms!"

Sharon hugged her harder. "Ernesto was shot," she said, swallowing the terrible words.

"That's not true!" Jada gasped.

Sharon's pained expression told the truth.

"Make it not be true," Jada said weakly.

"Tía Nina called me. She wondered where you were. She wondered if you were all right. I panicked. I thought you went to meet Ernesto and . . . "

Jada trembled. "Is he . . . ?"

"He's at Highland. I told her we'd come as soon as possible."

CHAPTER 30

Our Seed of Hope

As they drove through Oakland, Jada's eyes swept over the streets, the buildings, the parks. Everything around her was present time. *Her time.* Instead of the same old same old, she tried to look with fresh eyes. Not only look but *read* the world as they passed the old houses and new condos, bright murals and sidewalk memorials, garbage and gardens, bikes, buses, and homeless people. In the past, Jada never bothered to notice homeless people. They blended into the city like benches and sidewalks. They sat, walked, slept, and panhandled. They were "homeless." Now she saw they were different ages, colors, and shapes.

Like Auntie Yates said, *It's not right for people to call you one thing.*

"Do you know homeless people?" she asked Moms.

"They ride my bus every day. If it's rainy and cold, they ride for hours," Sharon said. "Some are crazy and need help. Others are the nicest, sanest people you ever met. You can't put folks in the same box. You hear what I'm saying?"

Jada remembered Ruthie's words: *It takes all of us, including you two.* But as Jada looked around, she wondered how she could ever make a difference.

They entered Highland through the emergency room. Jeannie Gray Dove Perry was at her desk.

"I took him to Tía Nina's house," she said when she saw them. "It's my fault."

Sharon patted Jeannie's hand. "You can't blame yourself."

"I do blame myself!" she said.

"Will he get better?" Jada asked.

"The doctors are hopeful," she said.

"We want to be near him," Sharon said.

Jeannie Perry directed them to the elevator. It was packed with friends and families of the sick, the injured, and the dying. *Everybody gets sick. Everybody has accidents. Everybody dies*, Jada thought. *But gun violence? It never has to happen.*

On the fifth floor, Sharon asked for information for Ernesto Cruz.

The nurse checked the chart. "He hasn't come up from surgery."

"We'd like to stay nearby," Sharon said.

"Are you family?"

"I'm his sister," Jada replied.

The nurse stared at Jada in disbelief. All afternoon, people had stopped by, claiming kinship with Ernesto Cruz. She believed the elderly Mexican lady and the boy named Leonard. But the Asian uncle, the black grandfather in a warmup suit, the young Middle Eastern cousin with her relatives, and now an African American girl insisting she was a sister?

"I give up on this mixed-up family!" the nurse said.

Jada whispered as they walked down the hall, "I don't like her."

"It's not easy work," Sharon sympathized. "It's the same on my bus. Sometimes you lose patience."

In the waiting room, Tía Nina rose to embrace them. Her smile was somber, and the sparkle in her eyes was dull. Jada hugged her tightly. Like Auntie Yates, Tía Nina was a rock. More than rock, she was a mountain.

Tía Nina introduced them to Mrs. Perry's son, Leonard; the boxing coach, Mr. Marvin; and Ernesto's

English teacher, Mr. Nok, who'd brought a stack of books. Then she came to the Syrian family.

"This is Amal," Tía Nina said. "She saved Ernesto's life."

Amal shook her head. "No, the medics saved his life," she said.

"Amal told him stories," Tía Nina said tearfully. "Sometimes it's a story that saves our life."

They met the other members of the Salim family. Amal's parents, her brother, and her sister had come to the hospital to check on Ernesto.

"Amal means *hope*," Tía Nina said. "When he got shot, Amal was there."

"He'll be coming up soon," Mr. Marvin said.

Jada sank into a chair and tried to make herself stop shaking.

"Where was he hit?" she asked fearfully. She knew even when bullets didn't kill, they changed lives forever.

"In the arm," Mr. Nok said.

Sokhom Nok had survived the genocide in Cambodia. He still had nightmares of guns, explosions, and mangled bodies. During the terror of the Khmer Rouge, areas of Cambodia were called "the killing fields."

"The brachial artery in his upper arm was severed," Amal's brother said.

"Amal took the ends of her scarf and tied off his arm," Tía Nina said.

"It wasn't my headscarf," Amal said. "My brother heard the shot and ran to us. He tied off Ernesto's arm with his belt."

"Or he would have bled to death," Tía Nina confirmed.

Once the ambulance arrived, the belt was replaced with a tourniquet. The medics called Highland to alert them to a Code 3 emergency. A team of trauma surgeons and emergency room doctors assembled to meet the ambulance, evaluate the wound, and decide on a course of action. The surgery was a delicate procedure. It required stitching Ernesto's artery together.

While they waited, Jada looked through the window at the treetops of East Oakland: the small, steep hills dotted with homes and apartment houses, large and small, old and new. In the near distance was a long row of tall, slender palms, a vestige of one of the grand estates that spread over this part of Oakland a hundred years ago.

"I am Dr. Bhandari," the surgeon announced.

Roopa Bhandari had cinnamon-colored skin and straight black hair. Her voice was calm and her manner serious and direct. It was impossible to tell if the news was good or bad.

"Who are the parents?" she inquired.

No one responded.

She glanced from face to face. "The mother or the father?" she asked.

"Ernesto is with me now," Tía Nina told her.

Dr. Bhandari shook hands with Tía Nina.

"He stays with me, too," Sharon said.

Dr. Bhandari shook hands with Sharon Yates.

"Me, too," Jada said.

Dr. Bhandari also shook hands with Jada.

To everyone's relief, the doctor said, "The operation went well. He'll make a full recovery."

Tears filled their eyes.

"He's a lucky boy in lots of ways. He's lucky to have all of you."

Jada jumped up. "Can we see him?"

"Not yet," the doctor said.

"I have something for Ernesto," Jada said, pulling a reddish-brown nut from her pocket. "Is it possible to give it to him after he wakes up?"

Dr. Bhandari held the acorn between her fingers. She examined the shiny shell and rough peaked cap. "To think that the mighty oak grows from such a tiny thing," she said. "I'll put it by his bed so he sees it as soon as he wakes up. Who shall I say brought it?"

"His soul sister," Jada said. "I have a message, too. Is that okay?"

"I can give him a message," Dr. Bhandari said.

"Tell him, *This acorn is our seed of hope.*"

Another Gift of Time

The next day, Jada rode the bus to the hospital.
From Fourteenth and Broadway, it was a short ride to
Highland. She signed in, got a visitor's badge, and rode
the elevator to the fifth floor.

"*¡Hola!*" Ernesto lit up at the sight of Jada.

She hugged his good arm. "*¡Hola, estúpido!*"

"Stupid or unlucky," he winced. "Either way, it's
bad."

She opened her backpack and pulled out a bag of
chips and two sodas.

"For you!" she said.

Ernesto's eyebrows lifted. "I'm not eating junk food
anymore!"

"Hey, I spent my own money!"

"Hey, I'm sorry! When you're on a sidewalk and think maybe you're dying, you make a vow. From now on, I'm taking care of myself."

Jada popped the cans and poured the liquid down the sink.

"I didn't tell you to dump it," he cried out.

"I'm taking the same vow!" Jada laughed.

"They want me to move around," he said, trying to sit up.

"If you can walk, we can visit Misty Horn. He's on the fifth floor, too."

Jada held his elbow and rolled his IV pole with bags of fluid towards the door. "Steady now," she said.

Ernesto rested his hand on her shoulder. Together, they took slow steps through the corridor to the cardiology department. Jada pushed on the door to Misty Horn's room.

Misty Horn gaped at Ernesto's bandaged arm, the sling, the hospital gown, the IV pole. "What happened to *you?*" he asked.

"Accident," Ernesto mumbled. "Wrong place, wrong time."

Misty Horn shook his head. "I don't believe it."

Ernesto touched his wounded arm. "I guess it really is *our* time."

Misty Horn motioned to his jacket in the closet. "I've got an idea," he said.

"You can't overexcite yourself," Jada warned.

"We'll be back in a jiffy," he promised.

"That's what you said last time!"

Nonetheless, she lifted the jacket from the hanger and carried it to Misty Horn. He reached into a pocket and lifted out a diminutive egg, smaller than the others with a window the size of a keyhole. As he held it in his palm, four numerals started to glow: **2-0-5-0**.

"The future!"

The harder we look, the more we see!
The more we stare, the sooner we get there!

Suddenly they found themselves elevated off the ground, hovering over the city, moving parallel to the Inner Harbor, east to west. It was an odd sensation, but they quickly got accustomed to floating.

Like outer space, Jada thought.

They recognized the hills, the shoreline, Lake Merritt, and landmark buildings. There were native plants on roofs and vertical gardens on walls along with promenades or *paseos* that connected sections of the city. Freeways had been converted to tree-lined bike and pedestrian boulevards with sleek jitney buses. Cars were no bigger than refrigerators with riders but no drivers. Where Grand Avenue used to be, a wide canal with water buses flowed from the lake to a ferry station under the Bay Bridge.

"When we humans were nomads, we traveled from place to place, foraging for food, water, and shelter," Misty Horn said.

"Like some Native tribes," Ernesto said.

"Nomads still exist, but many of us put down roots on farms and in villages. Villages are like acorns," Misty Horn smiled. "They sprouted into towns and cities, metropolises and megacities. Cities became overwhelmed by city problems: overcrowding, pollution, traffic, poverty, and alienation."

Jada thought of "aliens" in space movies. Ernesto thought of his immigrant parents.

"*Alienated* usually describes someone who feels cut off from others. That's not always a bad thing. An outsider's viewpoint can be most illuminating. But too often, those who are alienated are also angry, hurt, and confused. If alienation leads to violence, I don't have to tell you how it affects the community. You live it every day. In villages, people had ways to connect to each other. They knew when someone was in trouble."

"The past has already unfolded. The future is only a set of possibilities."

Jada touched Hishmen's abalone pendant around her neck. "West Oakland sometimes feels like a village with little villages inside it," she said.

"There have always been wonderful neighborhoods and communities in Oakland, but here are squares that link them. Inspired by the *zócalos* of Mexico, they are safe places to enjoy the gift of time."

"It's different," Ernesto observed, peering down.

"The people themselves made the difference. They had had enough."

"People had already had enough," Jada said, recalling Asante's shout *ENOUGH IS ENOUGH!*

"Oakland has lots of folks working for change. However, it still took time to recover from the violence and heal families and neighborhoods. Block by block and street by street, they succeeded."

"I like it," Jada said.

"Two gifted architects, Amal Salim and Ernesto Cruz, designed the squares."

"You're joking!" Ernesto exclaimed.

"The Ohlone showed you how beauty inspires beauty. If beauty surrounds us, it becomes the gift we give each other. If it's erased from the world, a light dies within us."

"When I got shot, I knew there was something I wanted to do if I lived," Ernesto said.

"Like give up junk food?" Jada grinned.

"I saw the past and future merge," Ernesto said. The past was flashes of Paco, Freddy, and the others who died on the street. The future was a dance of beautiful shapes and colors.

"Imagining a different world can be a matter of life and death," Misty Horn said.

Ernesto thought of Scheherazade in *Arabian Nights*. She imagined stories to save her life.

They floated over a tiled building. On the circular roof, *C.P.W.* was spelled out in flowers. Misty Horn's eyes twinkled. "That's the Center for Peace Warriors. They keep the peace."

"And the police?" Jada asked.

"Each community elects a committee to oversee safety, health, and security. Even school principals are elected. In that way, the community governs itself."

"Maybe my friend, Leonard Perry, started the C.P.W.," Ernesto said.

"Your friend *and* your enemy," Misty Horn said.

"Leonard was never my enemy!"

"And José Santiago?"

Ernesto clenched his teeth. "I hate him!"

"Me, too!" Jada said.

Misty Horn grew quiet. He didn't speak for a few minutes. Finally he said, "I understand why you feel that way. But hate is a vampire. When you hold onto it, hate sucks you dry."

"You don't really mean José Santiago," Ernesto said bitterly.

"Like places, people can change, too. Eventually José put his anger and hate behind him. He and Leonard created C.P.W. chapters all over the world. They helped kids claim a future without gangs, violence, drugs, and crime."

They floated down to the ground. Up and down the street were shops, restaurants, theaters, and clubs. Overhead was a glass tube for BART trains. An arch stretched across the street with the inscription:

WELCOME TO WEST
OAKLAND'S 7th STREET

"Hello, neighbor," people said as they passed.

"Hello, neighbor," Misty Horn said.

"Do you *know* them?" Jada asked.

"I don't have to know them. *Neighbor* means we're connected. *Neighbor* means we share something in common."

"Everybody seems relaxed," Ernesto said.

"They work less. They do what they love. There's more living green than gray concrete, so the earth can breathe. Humans can breathe, too. It was your generation who was determined to make a better world for everyone. Your generation went way outside the box."

Jada looked around. It was exciting to see the future. *But what about my big dreams?* she wondered. Maybe she'd dropped out of school. Or gotten lost like her Daddy.

"I guess you want to know about Dr. Yates," Misty Horn chuckled.

"Me?" Jada beamed.

"Jada Star Yates, Doctor of Astronomy, has worked on five continents, studied the universe, and made remarkable discoveries. She was inspired by educational systems she saw on her travels so she and her husband returned to Oakland to start a school."

"Her husband?" Jada blushed.

"Why not?" Misty Horn asked, but Jada didn't reply.

On the wall of the Sixteenth Street railroad station, Jada read a colorful, hand-painted sign:

STAR SCHOOL
Welcome Friends & Strangers!

They walked towards the renovated building. The antique windows were intact, but the roof was dotted with solar panels and the grounds filled with play structures. In front were rows of vegetables and fruit trees. Beyond the building was a forest as dense as the Oakland hills.

"We had urban farms in Oakland when I was young," Jada said.

"We're still young!" Ernesto chimed.

"Urban farms were part of the food solution, but they couldn't counter the waste in the entire system. Forty percent of the nation's food either spoiled or was thrown out. Now each block in Oakland has a corner lot to grow vegetables and fruit, raise chickens, collect rainwater, compost, and recycle."

Through the station's double doors, dozens of kids tumbled onto the grassy lawns and ball courts for morning exercises. Teachers exercised, too.

"You can't do anything if mind and body are separated," Misty Horn said.

"That's what my boxing coach tells us," Ernesto said.

"Like Oakland Community School," Jada said, remembering Ruthie's words: *Picture a light entering the bottom of your spine and rising through the crown of your head, shining positive energy.*

"Star School is about educating a total person: mind, body, and heart. There's an exchange of teaching and learning: students with teachers, teachers with students. Kids work out their own emotional problems, too," Misty Horn said.

Jada nodded with understanding. In sixth grade, she had been part of a "restorative healing circle." Young people shared their anger, frustration, shame, doubt, and despair. At first, it was hard for anyone to admit they had problems. Soon everybody wanted to discuss them. It was Jada's first chance to tell outsiders about her daddy. Nobody laughed. Nobody put anybody down. Sharing helped. It brought them together. It changed attitudes. It showed that given the chance, they cared about each other.

In the circle, they each made a "memory box" for the past and a "hope box" for the future. In her hope box, Jada put a photo of her daddy, Randolph Russell Yates. In her memory box, she put a photo of him, too.

"At Star School, students are asked to answer these essential questions:

Who am I?
What do I love?
How shall I live?
How can I make a difference?

"Answers change, but they are the students' yard-sticks about themselves and how they consider others. Everyone is expected to get along. That's called respect. Without it, we have no future."

Jada thought about the soup they had cooked and the bread they had baked after the earthquake. People spoke to strangers like family. Everybody got along, all colors, classes, ages. As Auntie Yates said, *Happiness is measured by what you give, not what you get.*

"Does Star School cost a fortune?" Ernesto asked.

"It's a free public school. Colleges and universities are free. Cost is no longer a barrier to a quality education."

From Sixteenth Street, they walked south under a canopy of oak trees. Birdsong flooded the air. A stream flowed near the path. Children skipped back and forth.

"Oaktown came back!"

"Every baby born in Oakland receives an acorn," Misty Horn said.

"When I was born, Moms got a little pink knitted hat!" Jada put that in her memory box, too.

"For your little brown head!" Ernesto teased.

"You're glad to have a hat in the rain and cold. But an oak tree is a magnificent thing all the time. It gives us oxygen and shade. It shelters us from storms. We can sit beside its trunk and play beneath its limbs. A tree is the future we leave to others."

Ernesto remembered Jada's message in the hospital: *This acorn is our seed of hope.*

"Is it okay to see this?" Jada asked.

"You warned Jada not to talk to Tommy Lee or Theresa Lyle. Or she might get stuck in another time," Ernesto said.

"There's a difference," Misty Horn said. "The past has already unfolded. The future is only a set of possibilities. It isn't written in a book or chiseled in stone. It's our hopes and dreams. It's up to us to make them real."

.

CHAPTER

The Stranger

On a chilly afternoon in late October, the doorbell rang. Jada wasn't expecting anyone. Kyra and Yasmine hadn't planned to come by. Her mother didn't mention visitors. Ernesto could have lost his key, but he knew where to find the spare under the flowerpot. Anyway friends and family never used the front door. They came down the driveway to the side of the house and entered through the kitchen.

"No, thank you!" Jada called through the attic window.

A man stepped off the front porch into the yard. "Hello!" he called back.

Jada darted away from the glass. She wasn't supposed to talk with strangers who came to the door. From experience, she knew if you ignored them long enough, strangers soon wandered away.

The doorbell echoed through the house again. She didn't like his persistence. Whatever he was selling, she didn't want it. If he was asking for money, she didn't have it.

She peeked through the window at the yard. The man sat beside the rosebush. He grinned, scratched his head, and wiped his eyes. *Grinning and crying?* Jada assumed he must be crazy. He hopped back to the porch and rang the bell a third time.

Jada reached for her phone, wondering if she should call Moms. Or Auntie Carol. Or Uncle Simon. Uncle Simon was calm in emergencies, calmer than Moms. He was also closer because he worked in downtown Oakland at the city's Parks and Recreation department.

Simon told her to go downstairs and check the doors. He said he'd be there in ten minutes. "If someone tries to break into the house, call 9-1-1," he said.

Jada crept down the two flights of stairs. She ducked when she passed the bay window and scooted down the hall to the kitchen. She checked the side door. It was locked. She checked the door in the utility room. It was locked, too. She went back to the living room and waited for Uncle Simon.

She listened to the tick of the grandfather clock. The familiar sound reminded her of the past, not Oakland's past but her family's past. Her family had more branches than she could count: those from Africa, those enslaved, those scattered around the country, those whose names she knew, those whose names were lost. It was a big responsibility to carry their hopes and dreams forward with her own. A big, big responsibility.

Through the front door, she heard a knock. "Jada Star!" the voice said.

Thank goodness! Uncle Simon had arrived in record time. She raced to the hall. When she flung open the door, there stood the stranger!

"Jada Star?" he asked tentatively.

"I don't know how you know my name! You get out of here right now!"

At that instant, Simon Yates jumped from his car. "Move away from her!" he yelled.

The stranger wheeled around to face Simon. Instead of a confrontation, Jada watched them fall into each other's arms. Hugging, kissing, crying, laughing, they held each other.

Simon slapped the stranger's back. "What about a phone call so I could pick you up? Better than sneaking around and scaring Jada to death!"

"I wasn't *that* scared," Jada said, ogling the stranger.

The two men laughed, cried, and hugged some more. Simon shouted to the neighborhood. "He's home! Randyman is home!"

Three words buzzed in Jada's head: *Randolph Russell Yates. Randolph Russell Yates. Randolph Russell Yates.*

"Jada, do you believe it?" Simon asked.

Jada could not believe it. It was the moment she'd waited for her whole life. But it wasn't real. It was surreal.

Jada stared at the stranger. Did she recognize him? Maybe his eyes or crooked front tooth. He certainly didn't resemble the high school photo in her memory box. Or fit the daddy of her distant memories. Or the soldier of her military fantasies. Or a prisoner.

"Jada Star!" Randy inhaled her name. "Let me look at you, baby girl. You are beautiful, outside and in. Pinch me so I know I'm not dreaming!"

Jada didn't want to pinch him, but he grabbed her fingers and pressed them on his arm.

"Daddy is *real!*" he shouted. "Flesh and blood real!"

Asking Forgiveness

Every couple of months, Sharon had visited Randyman in prison. In between, they kept in touch by phone. She knew he was coming home. She knew to expect him. Nevertheless, when she saw him on the front steps of the family house, sitting with Jada and Simon in the fresh air, dressed in jeans and a sweater, she bounded from the station wagon to the house and collapsed in Randy's arms.

Randy and Simon helped her into the living room. Jada ran to the kitchen for a glass of water. Tears began to flow from Sharon's eyes.

"Did you ever believe this day would come?" she cried.

"Long coming," Randy sighed.

"A lifetime," Sharon said.

Jada scrutinized her mother's face. Moms was often angry about something. Now she didn't look angry. Cuddled next to Randy, she looked tender and soft. Both of them looked happy. Moms and Randyman were together again.

"Come sit with us," Sharon said.

"There isn't room," Jada said.

Randy scooted over. "There's always room for you."

Jada frowned. "I'm going upstairs," she announced.

"Don't go!" Randy cried.

"I have homework," she said curtly.

"I guess I shouldn't interfere," Randy said.

"I guess not," Jada agreed.

She turned and dashed up to the attic. When she slammed the door, the noise reverberated throughout the house. She threw herself on the bed and sobbed into her pillow.

"Should I go to her?" Randy asked.

"Let her take her time," Sharon said. "She got used to thinking her biggest wish in the world would never happen. Now it has come true. That takes an adjustment."

In the evening, the family gathered on Wood Street for a celebration supper.

"Good to meet you," Randy told Ernesto. "I've heard so much about you."

"Your family has really helped me out," Ernesto said. "Someday I hope my *papá* and *mamá* can come back to Oakland. Right, Jada?"

Jada didn't respond.

"She isn't feeling well," Sharon said.

"Too much excitement," Auntie Yates added.

"Hey, what's up?" Ernesto asked Jada. He'd never seen her so glum.

"Leave me alone!" she blurted.

After dinner, Randy stood up. "I think you know what this means to me. On second thought, you don't have a clue."

Jada put her head down on the table, but she could feel her daddy's eyes drilling into her.

"I walked out of prison a changed man. That's how everyone walks out. For better and for worse, we're changed." Randy lifted a brown paper bag. "When I left, the prison returned the things I'd brought with me."

One by one, he pulled out items from the bag: his wallet with a library card, his expired driver's license, a few dollars, a movie ticket, chap stick, and mirror sunglasses.

"I didn't care about any of them except . . ."

Jada looked up.

Randy held a blue plastic key. "Anybody remember?"

Jada started to laugh. Her laughter cut through the tension in the room. Everybody broke into peals of laughter.

"What's the joke?" Ernesto asked although he was laughing, too.

"It's a key to Fairyland!" Jada said.

"It's not just a key," Randy said joyfully. "It's *our* key."

"I've never been to Fairyland," Ernesto said. "Is it funny?"

"Before I went away, Jada Star and I used to go every weekend."

Jada's lips trembled. Her eyes clouded. The memory was dim, but yes, she remembered Willie the Whale, the Clocktower Slide, the little farm, storybook characters, puppet shows, and the plastic key that unlocked the boxes that played nursery rhymes.

"It's a magic oasis," Misty Horn said.

"It's the first place I plan to go, but I need company. They don't let adults in without a child."

"I'm not a child anymore, Daddy," Jada protested.

"In that case, we'll take Auntie Carol's kids. You'll come along, won't you?"

Jada scrunched her face. "To Fairyland?"

"Can I come?" Ernesto asked.

"I'm going!" Misty Horn said.

Randy passed the key around the table.

"It's cute," Ernesto said.

"Maybe if you're in kindergarten!" Jada retorted.

Auntie Yates served the apple crumble. Sharon made tea. When they had settled down with dessert, Randy spoke again.

"I've got a few more things to say," he smiled bashfully. "Things I've waited to say a long time."

Everyone listened carefully. When Randy went to the prison, the heart of the family broke. Now the family was whole again.

"No matter what you do and where you go, a man learns to say, *I'm sorry.*"

"A woman, too," Sharon seconded.

"We learn we aren't perfect, life isn't perfect, and mistakes get made along the way." Like a compass, he turned to Jada. "First, I want to tell you I'm sorry that I caused you grief and pain. I let you all down, especially Sharon and Jada. I let my world down because I was *in there* instead of *out here.* Life is a two-way street.

You put in. You take out. When I wasn't strong enough to stay out of trouble, trouble took me down." Randy steadily held each person's gaze. "I hope you can find a place in your heart to forgive me."

Ernesto thought of Misty Horn's words: *Hate sucks you dry, but love gives you life.*

"Everybody knows that a good parent is supposed to protect their kids from harm and teach them to respect themselves and others. Lots of kids grow up never feeling safe or protected. They grow up without respect. As for me? I totaled zero as a dad."

"Randy," Sharon interrupted. "You don't have to do this now."

"I do," Randy said firmly.

Jada laid her head down again and sobbed silently, her back jerking up and down.

"In prison, you don't really live. You're suspended in a kind of slow death. The years are cold and lonely, always the same. Although I found ways to pass the time, I couldn't find peace." He reached out and took Sharon's hand. "She knows."

Jada dried her eyes on her sleeve. She peered up at her dad. *It must have been so hard for Moms*, she thought. *Cold and lonely for her, too.*

The room was quiet. The streets were quiet. No screeches, rumbles, sirens, or horns.

"Two years ago, a man from the Office of Victim Services contacted me in prison."

"Victim services?" Simon asked.

"It's part of the restorative justice program that offers contact to the victim of a crime with the perpetrator."

"Why would they want contact? To humiliate you?" Simon asked. "You went to prison! You paid for your crime!"

"Hear me out!" Randy demanded.

"You can't remake the past," Simon said.

"Maybe I *needed* to hear about his grief. Maybe I *needed* him to listen to me. Not my excuses but my state of mind and my regret. Maybe I was curious what would happen if we met as human beings outside a courtroom."

"Maybe you'd both start to heal," Auntie Yates murmured.

"That's why it's called 'restorative,'" Sharon said. "You hear what I'm saying?"

"I wasn't sure I could face him. Not only was I scared, but I was filled with guilt and shame. I had to think about it. For a year, Mr. Drummond and I met separately with Mike Adamson, our facilitator. When Mike thought we were ready, he set a date."

Randy looked at Auntie Yates. "*If we live in fear, we can never grow and change.* Isn't that what you told me?"

"It's what I tell everybody," Auntie Yates said.

"I can't imagine," Simon grimaced.

"It's about admitting you're sorry. You've done it a thousand times."

"Not like *that*," Simon said.

"Nothing could make up for the harm I caused Gabriel Drummond. But if I was going to take responsibility, shouldn't I know what the harm was?"

Randy steadied himself. He took a sip of tea. He brushed a tear from his cheek. He was hot and cold, sweaty and chilled.

"Late last year, Mr. Drummond came to the prison. I was shaking. I could barely walk through the door. As soon as I entered the conference room, I got the shock of my life. He hugged me. He didn't say anything. He just held me."

"That's intense," Simon whistled.

"It was the last thing I expected," Randy said. "When we finished hugging, Mike sat us down. He said the time had come. Didn't I know it! He asked for a minute of silence. A million thoughts whirled through my mind, but I told myself I could do it."

"Good job, Daddy!" Jada said softly.

She thought of her own restorative healing circle. After they talked over their problems, they felt close. Even if there had been conflicts in the past, they hugged each other, too.

"Mike asked Gabriel to speak about the pain in his arm and leg and the horrible headaches. I listened to him talk about his weeks in the hospital and months of physical therapy. As I listened, I repeated to myself, 'I caused this. I caused this.' When he finished, I acknowledged the harm and my remorse.

"Then Gabriel listened to me. I talked about my childhood, my hard-working parents, my siblings, my education, my marriage to the woman I loved, and our precious baby, Jada Star. I tried to explain how I got caught up in easy money, jeopardizing everything for a few bucks. I couldn't explain it even to myself. It was as if I had a breakdown. Instead of going crazy in my head, I went crazy in the street. Again I acknowledged the harm I caused him. I asked his forgiveness."

Ernesto wondered about the hate festering inside him. *Could he ever forgive José Santiago?*

"I can't undo what I did, but a great weight has lifted from both of us. Our next step was to make things as right as possible. We wrote out a pledge. I promised if I ever got the chance, I would make a positive contribution to my family and community."

"I guess your chance has come," Auntie Yates said.

New Beginnings

The next weekend, the family went to Fairyland. They sat by Lake Merritt with a picnic lunch, watching the boats glide over the water and the birds splash near the shore.

"Daddy!" Jada called. "Did you know that Lake Merritt was the first wildlife sanctuary in the United States?"

"You forget I'm an ignorant man!" he teased.

"Uncle Simon says you're the genius in the family," Jada said.

Randy pulled his younger brother's ear. "That's because your Uncle Simon is a blockhead!"

"When the *Californios* lived here, it was a marsh," Ernesto said. "It was called *Laguna Peralta.*"

"Ohlone came here to gather tule for their houses, boats, and clothes," Jada said.

"TU-LEE!" Ernesto slapped Jada five.

She untied the abalone pendant that Hishmen gave her. "Daddy, feel how smooth the edges are."

Whenever Jada said "Daddy," Randy's heart skipped a beat.

"It looks old," he said.

"It's ancient," she laughed, tying the ribbon around his neck. "You wear it."

"It came from a different time and place," Ernesto said.

"I believe it," Randy said, holding the polished abalone disc.

Ernesto pointed to the Camron-Stanford house. "That house is from another time and place, too. This lake was once encircled by houses like that and during the earthquake . . . ,"

"You mean Loma Prieta in 1989? You weren't even born!"

"I mean 1906 when tens of thousands left the ruins of San Francisco for Oakland. Many camped on the lake," Ernesto said.

"Many stayed and made Oakland their new home," Jada noted.

"Knowing your own history, that's a survival thing," Sharon said.

They sat by Lake Merritt with a picnic lunch, watching the boats glide over the water and the birds splash near the shore.

"Knowing the history of others lets us walk in *their* shoes," Auntie Yates said.

"Everything changes," Maisha philosophized.

"She *always* says that," Jada said.

It was a wonderful family outing. However in the weeks that followed, things did not go well for Randy Yates. He applied for jobs as a mechanic, a welder, a cook, and a custodian. He applied for whatever was available.

"I can do anything," he said in the interviews.

Some listened sympathetically, but no one hired him.

Randy's optimism ran out. His energy ran down. He was tired and irritable. He wondered if he'd have to pay for his crime for the rest of his life.

"I feel like they know I'm an ex-convict," he complained to Sharon. "How can I fight this prejudice?"

"The same way we always fought prejudice. You've got to join with others. You've got to make the change."

"I start thinking about the bias against gays and lesbians, disabled folks and seniors," Randy said.

"They joined up with each other. They made change happen," Sharon said.

"As a black man with a prison record, I don't stand a chance."

"At least you don't have to check the box on the job application," Sharon said.

"But if they ask the question, what am I supposed to say? You remember Glenn Burke? Black and gay, he refused to lie about himself. He was driven out of major league baseball," Randy said angrily.

"You'll find something," Sharon said. "There are caring people everywhere."

"The problem isn't people. It's the system that doesn't care."

"I hear you," Sharon said.

"When the Oakland Army Base was open, you could get a decent job," Randy complained. "Half my family worked there."

"Those years are long gone," Sharon said.

Jada was at the table, listening carefully. "Everything changes." She repeated what Maisha liked to say.

"What if it changes for the worse?" Randy said.

"You've got to stay positive," Sharon said.

"Ask Ernesto to take you to the gym," Jada suggested. "You can't do anything if your mind and body are disconnected."

"True, true," Sharon said to Randy. "She's a wise soul. Didn't I tell you?"

When Jada signed up for a restorative healing circle at school, the counselor asked her to be a circle leader. She encouraged Kyra and Yasmine to sign up, too.

Every Sunday, Tía Nina visited the house on Wood Street. She and Ernesto called his parents in Mexico. When Catalina Cruz heard about the shooting, she wanted to climb inside the trunk of a car and come to California. Carlos, her husband, dissuaded her. He wanted them to return legally.

In Oakland, Catalina Cruz never dared to speak out. For an undocumented immigrant, a dehumanizing job was better than no job. Living in California had given Catalina a sense of her own power and worth. Around her, ordinary women constantly spoke out. Maybe she would speak out, too.

Catalina heard about U visas. She found the information she needed on a neighbor's computer. At first, the I-918 form for the U visa overwhelmed her. Not only was it long but the questions brought back the bad memories of abuse she'd suffered from the boss of the AZ Tortilla Factory. Catalina had been the victim of several beatings. Proof were the scars on her arms and back and a medical report. The other women had been beaten, too. Some women had been kept locked up for days. The boss threatened to report them to *la migra* if they told anyone. Of course, no one said a word.

In addition, there was another form that certified Catalina's willingness to cooperate with the police. After she mailed the papers to the United States, she waited anxiously for a reply. Until she officially qualified as the victim of a crime, she couldn't travel to California. Finally, she received her certification. She was overjoyed that she'd soon see Ernesto. She was also proud that she might bring her old boss to justice.

She and Carlos didn't tell Ernesto their plans. If anything went wrong, they didn't want to disappoint him. In early December, after the weather had turned rainy and cold, they arrived in Oakland. They carried bags stuffed with coconut candy, sweet potato jam, salty cheese, and *adobo* seasoning. They also carried new hopes and dreams. Oakland was where their son had been born. Oakland was their son's home.

Tía Nina and Jorge picked them up at the airport. They drove directly to West Oakland. Like Randy, they came to the house on Wood Street unannounced. Sharon was at work. Jada and Ernesto were at school. Randy answered the door.

"Tía Nina," he greeted her. "What a surprise!"

"A big surprise!" she said, introducing him to Ernesto's parents.

"Ernesto didn't mention anything," Randy said.

"Until the airplane landed, we were worried they'd stop us," Catalina said.

"Welcome!" Randy shook their hands.

They came into the warm house. Randy made coffee and tea and served crackers and cheese. Every day, he did new things he hadn't done since he went to prison.

"Tell us, is he okay?" Catalina asked.

"Okay? Ernesto is great!" Randy said.

"After I left, there was trouble," Carlos said.

"I think the trouble is behind him," Randy said. "He and Jada are in a healing circle at school. It gives them a safe place to talk over problems and work out solutions with their peers."

"Healing circle," Catalina repeated. She thought the whole world needed a healing circle.

Five years had passed since Carlos had seen his son. During that time, he had tried not to worry. Suddenly he couldn't wait another minute. He checked his watch.

"I hope they get home soon," he said.

Outside, they heard laughter. "There they are!" Randy said.

"I'm so nervous," Catalina said.

Holding on to each other, Carlos and Catalina stepped into the front hall. As the key turned in the lock, they yanked on the door.

"*Mi corazón*," Catalina cried.

Ernesto pinched Jada. "Are we inside an egg?"

Catalina hugged Ernesto while Carlos wrapped his arms around both of them. They cried. When Sharon arrived home, she cried, too. Happiness makes sweet tears.

When the holidays came, there was much to celebrate, most of all reunion and love. In addition to family and old friends, many new friends were invited to the party on New Year's Day at the house on Wood Street: Leonard and Jeannie Gray Dove Perry; Mr. Nok, Ernesto's former English teacher, and his Swedish girlfriend; Mr. Marvin, Ernesto's boxing coach; Asante, their neighbor; Keesha Pine, the counselor for their restorative healing circle; and Amal Salim and her family. Everybody brought a favorite dish.

"To Janus, the Roman god of doors and gates, past and future, beginnings and endings! Happy New Year!" Misty Horn stood and cheered. He passed around a gold coin of Janus with two identical bearded faces in profile: one face looked backward and the other forward.

Jada and Ernesto glanced at each other with perfect understanding. Their past was not only their time. They shared it with Hishmen, the Peraltas, Johnny, Mr. Yuen, Li Hua, Tommy Lee Yates, and Ruthie.

All afternoon, the living room was pleasantly crowded, abuzz with conversations in several languages.

At five o'clock, as the grandfather clock chimed the hour, the door creaked open. A tall, hunched man limped into the living room. He waved apologetically.

"Sorry to be late," he croaked.

Sharon came forward. She took the man's overcoat and extended her hand. "Welcome," she said.

Randy bounced across the room. "Everybody, this is Mr. Drummond!" he shouted.

"Call me Gabe," he said.

"Hello, Gabe!" the crowd called out.

Gabe Drummond was handed a plate of food: black-eyed peas and rice, *markouk*, shrimp gumbo, and *thuk kreong*. Auntie Yates and Misty Horn made space for him on the horsehair sofa. They sat together, nibbling and discussing the state of the world. There was plenty to criticize, but they shared hopes for the coming year.

When Gabe Drummond rose to leave, he leaned on Randy's arm. They moved slowly to the front door.

"Yesterday, I had some news," he said.

"I hope it was good news," Randy said.

"That depends on you," Gabe smiled mysteriously.

"Me? I don't understand."

"I trust you completely," Gabe said.

"*You* trust me?" Randy stammered.

"I do," Gabe confirmed. "Do you trust me?"

"Of course!"

"So there you have it. Against all odds, we have each other's trust."

"What depends on me?" Randy questioned.

"Edith Bethel telephoned me about work. She heard about us."

"How in the world?" Randy asked in astonishment.

"I am as surprised as you are," Gabe said.

"Ms. Bethel thinks we have something important to say. She wants to hire us to say it."

"I'm laying low," Randy told Gabe. "Trying to keep my head above water and get back on my feet. I can't offer anything to anyone."

"Ms. Bethel thinks we ought to tell our story of crime and punishment, pain and grief, forgiveness and healing. She believes we can shift perceptions about who *you* are and who *I* am. Not *offender* and *victim* but many things: two people trying to move forward without hate, prejudice, and fear."

Randy scanned the wall of photographs: those who were stolen from Africa and enslaved, those who escaped Jim Crow and came to Oakland, those who traveled the country in the Pullman cars, those who fought in two world wars, those who marched and petitioned and battled for change.

"Give it some thought," Gabe said. "I believe our story is worth telling."

Randy closed the door. He listened to Gabriel Drummond's cane thump over the wooden boards of the old porch and down the stairs. He heard the car start and drive away. He replayed Gabe's words in his head: *our* story, *our* story, *our* story could change the world.

Soon other guests began to leave.

"Happy New Year," they said as they hugged each other.

"Happy New Year," they called.

"It was a wonderful party!" Randy said.

"Everyone had a wonderful time!" Sharon happily agreed.

"*Felíz Año Nuevo*," Catalina and Carlos said.

Jada and Ernesto smiled at their parents. Two broken circles had mended.

Who am I? Jada whispered to him. *How shall I live?*

What do I love? Ernesto whispered in return. *How can I make a difference?*

Awaiting them were clues from the past and future. But today was present time. *Their time.* A day they would remember for the rest of their lives.

THE END

APPENDIX

For the full appendix and bibliography, see **www.oaklandtales.com**.

For information on walking tours, contact the **City of Oakland** at (510) 238-3234 and www.oaklandnet.com/walkingtours; **Oakland Heritage Alliance (OHA)** at (510) 763-9218 and www. oaklandheritage.org. Visit the **Oakland Museum of California**, 1000 Oak Street, Oakland, CA 94607 (free admission on the first Sunday of the month). **Oakland History Room,** Oakland Public Library at 125 Fourteenth Street, has books, maps, files, and photographs of Oakland's history.

9-11 references the September 11, 2001 attacks on the World Trade Center and the Pentagon. In the aftermath of 9-11, hostility against Arab Americans escalated.

442nd Regimental Combat Team (U.S. Army) was a fighting unit composed mostly of American soldiers of Japanese descent who volunteered to fight in World War II although their families were subject to internment.

Afro-Latino is a person of African and Spanish descent. The last *Californio* governor, Pio Pico, was an Afro-Latino. See also *Californio.*

Alameda was once a peninsula of Oakland and later separated by an estuary.

Alcatraz Island is located in San Francisco Bay. It is often called "The Rock." From 1933-1963, it was a federal prison. After the prison was closed, the island was declared "surplus federal property." Inspired by old treaty agreements regarding federal property, Native Americans occupied Alcatraz Island from November 1969 to June 1971. Each November on the fourth Thursday, a dawn ceremony is held on Alcatraz Island to celebrate the rights of indigenous people and Unthanksgiving Day.

Alta California ("Upper California") is today's state of California. It was once part of the Spanish Empire. After Mexico's War for Independence, it was part of Mexico until 1848.

Angel Island in San Francisco Bay functioned as a U.S. detention center for immigrants (1910-1940), especially Asians. Sometimes detainees remained for years. Poems of despair were written and carved onto the barrack walls (visible today). Contact (415) 435-5537 and tours.angelisland@parks.ca.gov. See also *Chinese.*

Anza expeditions were two expeditions led by Juan Bautista de Anza to *Alta California* from Mexico (1774 and 1775) to establish a permanent presence. The route started in the Sonoran Desert and traveled through Arizona west to the Pacific coast. The **Peralta Hacienda Historical Park at 2465 Thirty-Fourth Avenue** (Fruitvale district of Oakland) is on the Juan Bautista de Anza National Trail. See also *Peralta family.*

Ban the Box is a movement to eliminate questions about arrests, convictions, and incarcerations from job applications.

Baó is a traditional black skullcap with a topknot worn by Chinese men for centuries.

Bay Area Negro Chorus was founded in 1935 by William Elmer Keeton and originally known as the Oakland Colored Chorus.

Beer gardens were outdoor drinking establishments owned and operated by Germans who settled in the Upper Fruitvale and Dimond districts in the late nineteenth century.

Berm is a small, earthen, dike-like embankment.

Beulah Heights is an area of East Oakland near Mills College where a cluster of charitable institutions settled in the late nineteenth century, including Home for the Aged and Infirm Colored People (1897-1938). The home was located on what is now part of Mills College.

Black Panther Party (BPP) was co-founded by Huey Newton and Bobby Seale in 1966 in Oakland. The party's original name was the Black Panther Party for Self-Defense. *Self-defense* was a term that addressed defense *against* assault of outside forces like police as well as defense *from* poverty, hunger, and joblessness. The BPP built on the significant victories of the Civil Rights movement while recognizing that legislation did not guarantee full equality. From its inception, the BPP slogan "All Power to

All the People" championed inclusiveness of race, class, and gender equality. The BPP's Ten-Point Program was created by Huey Newton and Bobby Seale. See wikipedia.org/wiki/ Black_Panther_Party

This small group of revolutionary activists founded a network of free "community survival programs" to provide basic needs, including free breakfast for schoolchildren, a free medical clinic, senior services, a school, a weekly newspaper, and many more. Within two years, 45 BPP chapters had sprung up across the country.

Visit **BPP historical markers on Market at 55th Street**, the corner of the first BPP community action, which resulted in the installation of a traffic light, and **5622 Martin Luther King Jr. Way**, the site of the first BPP office. Information for **Black Panther tours of West Oakland** at **blackpanthertours.com**

See also *Alcatraz Island* for Red Power, *Brown Berets* for Brown Power, *COINTELPRO, International Hotel* for Asian Power.

Black Panthers' Free Breakfast Program for Schoolchildren ensured that local children had breakfast before school. In January 1969, the first breakfast program was established in West Oakland. It was the model for the federal free/reduced breakfast/lunch programs that now serve low-income youth in the public schools.

Black Panthers' Free Health Clinic provided check-ups, immunizations, and information on sickle cell anemia, lead poisoning, and nutrition, as well as door-to-door services.

Black Panthers' Oakland Community School (OCS) was founded in 1974 at **6118 East Fourteenth Street** (now International Boulevard) near Seminary Avenue. OCS enrollment included students from the entire community.

Black Panthers' S.A.F.E. (Seniors Against a Fearful Environment) program provided escort services to seniors, meals (predecessor of "Meals on Wheels"), and buses to prisons on visitor days.

Bracero (Spanish for "manual laborer," *brazo* means arm) program provided temporary contract laborers from Mexico to work in the United States (1942-1964).

Brooklyn was an early name for the part of East Oakland between Lake Merritt and about Twenty-Third Avenue.

Brotherhood of Sleeping Car Porters (BSCP) was a union of Pullman porters organized in 1925 with the motto *Fight or Be Slaves.* Pullman was the largest employer of blacks in the country (in 1926, there were 12,000 porters and waiters). When the company started, it hired former slaves who were well-mannered and accustomed to servitude. For decades, the Brotherhood tried to organize for higher pay, better work conditions, and the end of discrimination and segregation practices. While porter was one of the best jobs available for African American men, it furthered the stereotype of "servant class."

A. Philip Randolph was the founder of the BSCP (the original name included "Maids"). C. L. Dellums was a Pullman porter in Oakland and BSCP's West Coast organizer. In 1929, he was elected the union's vice president, a position he held until 1968 when he succeeded Mr. Randolph as president. BSCP's headquarters was at **1716 Seventh Street** in West Oakland. Today, a statue of C.L. Dellums stands at the **Oakland Amtrak station** (in Jack London Square). See also *Pullman Palace Car Company.*

Brown Berets was a Chicano/Mexican American community organization that emerged during the Chicano Movement in the late 1960s and was active in the Fruitvale district of Oakland. See also *Black Panther Party.*

Brown, Dr. Beth A. (1969-2008) was an African-American astrophysicist at NASA's Goddard Space Flight Center.

Brown lung is a respiratory disease caused by breathing organic matter, common in the textile industry.

Bullfight typically describes a fight between a bull and a *matador* (a person trained to fight bulls). During the *Californio* period, sometimes bulls fought bears. There were at least two bullrings in East Oakland, one at the **Peralta's** *rancho* **(2465 Thirty-Fourth Avenue)** and another at the current site of **San Antonio Park (1701 East Nineteenth Street between Seventeenth and Eighteenth Avenues)**. Although a native of Hawaii, William Heath Davis (1822-1909) contributed greatly to our understanding of early California in his book, *Seventy-Five Years in California.*

Burke, Glenn (1952-1995) played major league baseball for the Dodgers and As, the first and only major league player known to come out as gay during his professional career.

California is a fictional place in a sixteenth-century fantasy novel by Garci Rodríguez de Montalvo. Today's California was originally part of a vast colonial empire called New Spain.

California Cotton Mill (**1091 Calcot Place next to I-880**) began operation in 1883 in the Fruitvale district and was a major employer and industry of national importance.

Californios were inhabitants of *Alta California* and like the Peraltas, descended from Spanish-speaking settlers from New Spain and Mexico. The *Californio* period starts in the late 1700s with the Anza expeditions and the establishment of the missions and ends with the U.S.-Mexican War in 1848. See also *Afro-Latino*, *Alta California*, and *Anza expeditions*.

Cambodian genocide occurred under the rule of the Khmer Rouge (1975–1979). Approximately two million Cambodians died from political executions, disease, starvation, and forced labor.

Cannery is a place where fruit, vegetables, fish, and other edibles are canned. In 1868, Josiah Lusk opened the first cannery on the banks of **Temescal Creek in the Claremont district of North Oakland**. By the 1880s, it was said to be the largest cannery west of the Mississippi. The Pacific Coast Canning Company was owned by Lew Hing and located at **Twelth and Pine Streets**. By the 1940s, the East Bay had an estimated 72 canneries. See also *Orchard*.

Carreta is a two-wheeled oxcart.

Chabot Space & Science Center is successor to the Chabot Observatory founded in 1883 at Eleventh and Jefferson Streets. The telescopes at Chabot Space & Science Center are: Leah, an 8-inch refractor type (acquired 1883), Rachel, 20-inch refracting type (acquired 1915), and Nellie, a modern 38-inch reflector type (acquired 2003). The Chabot Observatory first moved to Mountain Boulevard because of light pollution and later to **10000 Skyline Boulevard. On Friday and Saturday evenings, the telescopes are open and free to the public** (weather permitting). Information at **www.chabotspace.org** and **(510) 336-7300**.

Charro is a Mexican horseman or cowboy who typically wears an elaborate outfit.

Child labor laws prohibit or regulate employment of underage children. The first child labor law in California was approved in January 1905. In 1910, over two million U.S. children were still employed (rolling cigarettes, engaged in factory work, working in textile mills, laboring in coal mines, canneries and on farms). See also *Doffer.*

Chinese men by the thousands left China in the mid-1800s because of famine, economic hardship, and civil war. They flocked to *Gam Saan* or "Gold Mountain" in the United States to work in the mining fields and on the railroads among other vocations. While the transcontinental railroad was under construction, railroad executives advocated for an unlimited immigration policy, only to be reversed after the railroad was completed. The Chinese built the earthen dams for Oakland's early water supply at Lake Temescal and Lake Chabot. Several times, Chinese were forced to leave one locale for another, finally settling at **Webster and Eighth Streets** in the 1870s. Despite prejudice and hardship, there were many successful Chinese in early Oakland. Visit **Hall of Pioneers, Harrison Square, 275 Seventh Street, Oakland Chinatown.** Visit **"Chinese Workers and the East Bay's Early Water System," EBMUD, 375 Eleventh Street, Oakland.** Free and open to the public. See also *Transcontinental railroad.*

Chinese Exclusion Act of 1882 restricted immigration. Exclusion or limited quotas for other Asian nationalities followed. After the 1906 earthquake destroyed many official records, Chinese in the United States were able to claim "paper" relatives. However, new Chinese arrivals were detained, imprisoned, and interrogated for months or even years on Angel Island. The *Chinese Exclusion Act* was repealed in 1943 when the United States and China were allies during World War II. See also *Angel Island.*

Chochenyo is one of eight related Ohlone languages spoken from Fremont to Richmond.

COINTELPRO (Counter Intelligence Program) was a secret program, sponsored by the FBI and designed to undermine, harass, destroy, and even murder members of a variety of student, leftist, and antiwar organizations, including the Black Panther Party.

Condor (California Condor or *Gymnogyps californianus*) is the largest flying land bird in North America.

Couves is kale or collard greens in Portuguese.

Coyote is a person who smuggles immigrants into the United States, especially across the Mexican border.

Damascus is the capital of Syria.

Deep South is part of the southeastern section of the United States. There was slavery in the Upper South and Deep South, but conditions were often more brutal in the Deep South where cotton and sugarcane were grown. See also *Jim Crow laws*.

Doffer is a worker in a cotton mill who replaces bobbins/cones on carding machines.

Double-V campaign was launched to bring attention to racist U.S. laws and attitudes against African Americans, even as thousands enlisted in the military to fight in World War II. The campaign was an important step in the full-blown Civil Rights movement a decade later. The campaign was initiated by a letter sent to the editor of the *Pittsburgh Courier* by James G. Thompson from Wichita, Kansas. Published on January 31, 1942 and on April 11, 1942, it openly questioned the sacrifice of life and limb to the cause of a country who didn't recognize "colored Americans" as full citizens. The Double-V campaign evolved from Mr. Thompson's letter and the *Pittsburgh Courier* staff artist, Wilbert L. Holloway, who created the visuals for the campaign.

Earthen dams were built by Chinese workers to create Oakland's Temescal and Chabot reservoirs. See also *Chinese*.

Embarcadero is a pier, wharf, or landing place, especially on a river or inland waterway.

Erhu is a Chinese violin with two strings.

Executive Order 8802, Prohibition of Discrimination in the Defense Industry, issued in June 1941, banned discriminatory employment practices in war-related work. See also *Rosie*.

Executive Order 9066. See *Internment camps.*

Fairyland is a children's amusement park and beloved **Oakland landmark beside Lake Merritt.** It opened in September 1950. Information at www.fairylandinfo@fairyland.org and (510) 452-2259.

Fandango is a dance party as well as a lively Spanish dance, popular with *Californios.*

Farm workers in California are mostly migrant workers, usually working under harsh conditions for low wages. For many decades, Mexican and Filipino workers tried to organize for workers' rights. In September 1965, the Agricultural Workers Organizing Committee (Filipinos) was the first to strike in the grape fields of Delano, California. Thirty percent of grape workers were Filipinos. Several weeks later, Cesar Chavez's National Farm Workers (Mexicans) joined them to form the United Farm Workers (UFW). See also *Filipino* and *Union.*

Feathered hats were very fashionable in the late nineteenth and early twentieth centuries. **Mr. Bentley's Ostrich Farm on East Fourteenth and High Streets** housed ostriches and a showroom. The number of wild birds slaughtered in the United States for hat decoration was staggering (a conservative report in 1886 estimated five million birds a year).

Feng Ru (1883-1912) migrated from China to San Francisco. In Oakland, he founded an "aeroplane" factory. His inaugural test flight in Oakland on September 21, 1909 was probably the first flight on the West Coast.

Filipino people claimed independence of the Philippine islands from Spain in 1898, only to be colonized by the United States in the Spanish-American War (1898-1902). Filipino immigrants flocked to the United States and like other Asians, faced hostility and discrimination. In World War II, there were special Filipino fighting units (200,000 fought and over half died). However, Congress denied Filipino soldiers their full military benefits. See also *Farm workers.*

Four [essential] questions: "Who am I? What do I love? How shall I live? How can I make a difference?" is quoted from *How Then Shall We Live? Four Simple Questions That Reveal the Beauty and*

Meaning of Our Lives. (Author's source: Benard, Bonnie. *Resiliency – What We Have Learned.* San Francisco: WestEd, 2004.)

Freedom papers were documents that had to be carried by freed slaves at all times to ward off slave-catchers and bounty hunters.

Gam Saan (also "Gum Shan," "Gumshan") or "Gold Mountain" is how Chinese referred to California after gold was discovered.

Gamen means "giving up" in Japanese although in the internment camps it was transformed into "bearing up." The art created in the camps was called "gamen." See also *Internment camps.*

Geta is a Japanese wooden shoe or clog.

Goat Island was once a name for Yerba Buena Island in the San Francisco Bay.

Golden Gate is the strait that connects San Francisco Bay and the Pacific Ocean. The Golden Gate Bridge was completed in 1937.

Grizzly bears (California Grizzly or *Ursus arctos californicus*) were everywhere in California until they were hunted into extinction.

Great Depression was a worldwide economic depression with mass unemployment, beginning with the 1929 stock market crash and continuing through the 1930s.

Heinold's First and Last Chance is a bar and eatery located at the foot of **Webster Street in Oakland's Jack London Square** and constructed circa 1880 allegedly from an old whaling ship.

Hide and tallow trade. Ships from around the globe swapped finished goods in exchange for California's hides (dried animal skins) and tallow (melted animal fat used to make candles). Cattle hides and vast tracts of land were the source of the Peraltas' wealth. Cattle hides were called "California dollars."

Hijab is a head scarf worn by Muslim women.

Horseless carriage was a name for early automobiles that ran on gas, steam, and electricity.

I AM AN AMERICAN is a photograph by Dorothea Lange, taken in March 1942, of a sign on a store window at **Eighth and Franklin Streets, Oakland.** The corner grocery store was owned by a Japanese American.

ICE is an acronym for the Immigration and Customs Enforcement Agency.

Idora Park was a seventeen-acre amusement park in North Oakland (**56th-58th Streets between Telegraph and Shattuck**) owned and operated by the Realty Syndicate from 1904-1929. See also *Key Route*.

Indian is the English translation of *indio*, used by the Spanish for all Native Americans. Anthropologist Alfred L. Kroeber estimated 133,000 Native Californians in 1770. By 1900, the population had been reduced to 25,000. A majority died from disease, but they were also enslaved, massacred, and chased off their lands. Instead of "Indian," many indigenous peoples prefer to be known as "Native American" or "First Nations people." Watch **INJUNUITY, a series of animated films** about contemporary Native American life and reflections on the past and future at **www.injunuity.org.**

Indian Relocation Act of 1956 encouraged and coerced Native Americans to leave reservations and move to urban centers to acquire vocational skills and assimilate into the general population. The government gave one-way bus tickets and many promises, too often broken. The 2000 California census counted 250,000 Native Americans with only 12% from indigenous California tribes. See also *Alcatraz Island* and *Intertribal Friendship House.*

Indio is Spanish for "Indian."

International Hotel or *I-Hotel* in San Francisco was a residential hotel, mostly occupied by Filipino men. Threat of eviction and demolition became a flashpoint for Asian and Asian-American activism. With much resistance, eviction occurred on August 4, 1977.

*Internment camp*s imprisoned approximately 120,000 Japanese and Japanese Americans (called "enemy aliens") in reaction to the December 7, 1941 attack on Pearl Harbor, Hawaii by the Japanese military. Executive Order 9066 was signed by President Franklin D. Roosevelt on February 19, 1942, leading to the removal from the West Coast of anyone with one-sixteenth Japanese ancestry. By summer 1942, there were permanent internment camps located in remote areas with harsh environments and poorly constructed housing, surrounded by barbed wire and guarded by military police. Most Japanese Americans from Oakland were sent to Topaz, Utah. The average stay in the camps was three to four years. In 1988, the U.S. government issued an apology to 82,000 surviving internees and reparations of $20,000 for each internee. Citizens and residents of German and Italian ancestry were also required to leave coastal areas but were not confined in camps. See also *Topaz.*

Intertribal Friendship House at **523 International Boulevard** was founded in 1955 by the American Friends Service Committee as one of the first urban Native American centers in the country, providing a place to gather for thousands of Native newcomers. The Bay Area has the fourth largest population of Native peoples in the United States. Information on community events at **www.ifhurbanrez.org**. See also *Native American Health Center.*

Janus is the ancient Roman god of transitions: gates, beginnings and endings, war and peace. The Romans named the month of January (*Ianuarius*) in his honor.

Jemison, Dr. Mae C. (b. 1956) is the fifth African-American astronaut and first African-American female astronaut in NASA history.

Jingletown is an area of East Oakland on the estuary near the California Cotton Mill and canneries. It was largely a Portuguese neighborhood and later became predominantly Mexican.

Jim Crow laws were state and local laws in the southeastern United States, mandating racial segregation in public facilities. These laws went into effect in the 1870s and were not overturned until the 1950s and 1960s. Segregated facilities and restrictions for blacks also existed in other parts of the country, including California. The U.S. military was segregated until Executive Order 9981 (July 26, 1948) abolished racial discrimination in the armed forces.

Kaiser shipyards in Richmond were the nation's largest shipyards (90,000 workers). Kaiser revolutionized ship manufacturing by prefabricating sections of ships and welding them together. During World War II, the Richmond shipyards broke two significant records: building more ships than any other U.S. shipyard (747); and building a ship in the fastest time on record of 4 days, 15 hours, and 26 minutes.

To transport workers, there was the "Shipyard Railway" between Oakland and Richmond. Kaiser also adopted the pioneering medical model of Dr. Sidney Garfield, the first voluntary group medical insurance plan that cost fifty cents a week. Childcare cost fifty cents a day. Kaiser hired many women and African Americans. Despite Executive Order 8802, there were discriminatory practices against women and workers of color at all shipyards. Visit **Rosie the Riveter WWII Home Front National Historical Park, 1414 Harbor Way South, Richmond, California**. Information at **(510) 232-5050**. See also *Rosie*.

KDIA was a black-oriented radio sation at 1310 AM, synonymous with soul music during the Black Panther era.

Key Route (later *Key System*) was a transit system based in Oakland and extending to other parts of the East Bay and San Francisco. It was owned and operated by the Realty Syndicate of Francis Marion "Borax" Smith and Frank C. Havens. In addition to streetcars, the Key System operated commuter trains that traveled on a *berm* or *mole* into the San Francisco Bay where ferry boats waited to transport passengers to San Francisco. Before the popularity of automobiles, 1,600 streetcars and trains ran daily in and around Oakland. See also *Berm* and *Mole*.

KPFA (94.1 FM), a listener-supported radio station, was founded in April 1949 in the aftermath of World War II by pacifists and conscientious objectors. It's part of the Pacifica Foundation.

La migra is a common term in the Latino community for the Immigration and Customs Enforcement Agency (ICE).

Lake Merritt was once a marsh. Several large creeks poured down from the Oakland hills, and seawater flowed in with tides from the Bay. As Oakland's population grew, the marsh acted as a sewer and was especially unpleasant for nearby residents. Mayor Samuel Merritt constructed a dam (1868-1869) which created Lake Merritt. It attracted large numbers of migratory birds. To protect the birds, Mayor Merritt had the lake declared a game refuge in 1870, the first such refuge in the United States.

Lupin or *lupini* is a large bean.

Macadam is a kind of road construction made with crushed stones and bound with tar or asphalt.

Mansion is a large, impressive house. Lake Merritt was once surrounded by mansions, oak trees, and gardens. To visit, check for information on tours and public access. The *Camron-Stanford House* stands at **1418 Lakeside Drive**. The *Cohen-Bray House* (1884) is at **1440 Twenty-Ninth Avenue** in East Oakland. The *Dunsmuir House and Gardens* is at **2960 Peralta Oaks Court**. The *Pardee Home Museum* at **Castro and Eleventh Streets** was home of the former mayor of Oakland and State Senator Enoch Pardee and his son George Pardee, governor of California. *Preservation Park* is a collection of sixteen historic houses at **Thirteenth Street and Martin Luther King Jr. Way.**

Marcus Books, a long-established bookstore with an African-American focus, was founded in San Francisco in 1960. A second store opened in Oakland in 1976 at **3900 Martin Luther King Jr. Way**. Information at **www.marcusbookstores.com** and **(510) 652-2344**.

Markouk is Middle Eastern flatbread, similar to pita.

Memory boxes and *hope boxes* are part of Amelie Prescott's art-and-healing program at the Dr. Martin Luther King Jr. Charter School in the Lower Ninth Ward, New Orleans. Information at **www.moschukmainstitute.org**.

Mexican War of Independence ended in 1821 and established Mexico as a nation. The new country abolished slavery.

Middle Harbor Shoreline Park at **2777 Middle Harbor Road** is located towards the west end of Seventh Street.

Military bases active in the Oakland area during World War II were Alameda Naval Air Station, Oakland Army Base, and Oakland Naval Supply Base. Segregation in the military was enforced until after World War II. See also *Jim Crow laws* and *Oakland Army Base*.

Missions of *Alta California* were vast agricultural tracts with churches at the center, established to convert the indigenous people to Christianity. Native American converts farmed the missions' land and tended the missions' herds. Under Spanish/Mexican rule, twenty-one missions were built one day's walk apart from San Diego to Sonoma (1769-1823). See also *Alta California*.

Mitchell, Maria (1818-1889) was a woman astronomer, born in Nantucket, Massachusetts.

Mochi is a sticky Japanese rice cake.

Mole is a solid structure (like a berm) that serves as a pier or break-water or causeway from the shore into the water. The Southern Pacific (SP) mole stretched almost two miles from the end of Seventh Street into San Francisco Bay where passengers would embark for a ferry to San Francisco. Some ferries were large enough to carry loaded freight cars. **Port View Park at the end of Seventh Street** is on the site of the SP terminal. The Key Route mole extended 3.26 miles into San Francisco Bay.

"Mongolian" was used as a derogatory term for Asians, especially Chinese.

Moore Dry Dock Company was located at the **foot of Adeline Street** after 1909. It was very active building and repairing ships during World War I and World War II (37,000 workers).

Mountain View Cemetery was built in 1863 at **5000 Piedmont Avenue in North Oakland. Free Saturday tours** are available twice a month, often with special themes. Information at **(510) 658-2588** and **www.mountainviewcemetery.org**. Also visit *Chapel of the Chimes* at **4499 Piedmont Avenue.**

Native American Health Center (NAHC) provides "comprehensive services to improve the health and well-being of American Indians, Alaska Natives, and residents of the surrounding communities, with respect for cultural and linguistic differences." It was founded in 1972 and is located at **3124 International Boulevard** in the Fruitvale district. Information on community events at **www.nativehealth.org**.

Navigation Trees (also called *Landmark Trees*) were used by European ships as a guide around Blossom Rock in San Francisco Bay. The trees were ancient giants: over 33 feet wide, 300 feet high, and 2,000 years old. They were logged around 1851. The historical marker is in **Madrone Picnic Area, Roberts Regional Recreation Area, Redwood Regional Park, 11500 Skyline Boulevard, Oakland.**

New Deal was a series of programs developed in President Franklin D. Roosevelt's administration to address the effects of the Great Depression, especially poverty, hunger, and unemployment. Oakland sites built during the New Deal include Alameda County Courthouse, Woodminster Amphitheater and Cascade, High Street Bridge, Caldecott Tunnel, Sausal Creek culverts, Morcom Rose Garden, Arroyo Viejo Park, Lake Temescal Beach House, Piedmont Elementary School, Chabot Elementary School addition, Sherman Elementary School, Roosevelt Middle School, and Fremont High School. See also *Great Depression*.

Oak trees defined the forest and woodlands of California. Twenty different types of oaks are native to the state. The single oak tree most associated with Oakland grows in front of City Hall, a coast live oak planted in 1916 in honor of Jack London. In the early mapping of the Bay Area, no site was as dense with oak forest as the shoreline and center of Oakland, hence the city's name. Watch **Saving the Bay - The Oaks of Oakland** at **http://www.youtube.com/watch?v=j7O3kKzfHn8.**

Oakland was founded in 1852. The first city plan laid out seven squares filled with oak trees. Visit **Jefferson Square, Harrison Square, Lafayette Square, Lincoln Square, and Madison Square**.

Oakland Airport was built in 1927. At the time, it claimed to have the longest runway in the world and the most modern airfield in the United States. Such a long runway enabled safe takeoffs for fuel-heavy aircraft. Several important historic flights began or ended in Oakland, including flights of Amelia Earhart.

Oakland Army Base (OAB) was "home to the largest military port complex in the world." During World War II, tens of thousands of troops and at least twenty-five million tons of supplies passed through OAB to the Pacific. Not only military personnel but thousands of civilians worked at the OAB and other Bay Area military bases. OAB was active during the Korean War, Vietnam War, and Gulf War. OAB's closure had a detrimental economic impact on the city, especially West Oakland, where it had provided well-paying jobs. **Entrance at 1400 Maritime Street.**

Oakland Larks was part of the all-Negro West Coast Baseball Association (WCBA) founded in 1945.

Oakland Oaks, nicknamed the Acorns, was a minor league baseball team and part of the Pacific Coast League.

Oakland Public Library opened as the Oakland Free Library on November 7, 1878, the second public library in California. The first Main Library (1878-1902) was on Fourteenth Street at the site of the present City Hall. The second Main Library (1902-1951) stands at **Fourteenth Street and Martin Luther King Jr. Way**, now home of the **African American Museum and Library at Oakland (AAMLO)**. The present **Main Library** between **Thirteenth and Fourteenth and Oak and Madison Streets** opened in 1951.

Ohlone is the Native American confederation of small tribes that lived for 2,500 years in the Bay Area from the Carquinez Straits to the Monterey area, including Oakland. Also called *Costanoan*, Native Americans inhabited the area without interruption for approximately 15,000 years, living in small communities with 60-100 inhabitants. Language and customs often varied.

With the arrival of the Spanish, the Ohlone way of life was destroyed. European diseases (like measles) ravaged the population. Spanish cattle and horses ruined the plant cycle of grasses. To survive, the Ohlone worked at the missions, *ranchos*, and *pueblos*. After the U.S.-Mexican War (1848), the Ohlones were generally treated worse by Americans than by *Californios*. California was a "free" state. However, there was de facto enslavement of Native Americans. Forced off their land by miners, ranchers, and farmers, many were sent to reservations and *rancherías*. None of the Ohlone tribes has federal recognition. However, some are seeking it. Watch **INJUNUITY, a series of animated films** about contemporary Native American life and reflections on the past and future at **www.injunuity.org**. See also *Shellmounds*.

Okie and *Arkie* were derogatory names for migrants from Oklahoma and Arkansas, states associated with the Dust Bowl, a severe drought that occurred in the United States during the 1930s. See also *Great Depression*.

Orchard is an agricultural area to grow fruit and nut trees. Henderson Luelling transported 700 Bing cherry trees overland for 2,000 miles to East Oakland and in 1856 planted them beside Sausal Creek. He called the area Fruit Vale (later Fruitvale).

Frederick Rhoda, another East Oakland pioneer, planted 2,000 Royal Ann cherry trees in 1859. See also *Cannery.*

Orphan is a child whose parents are dead or unable to raise their child. From 1901-1913, Mary R. Smith (first wife of F. M. "Borax" Smith) founded the Mary R. Smith's Trust for Orphan Children. Cottages with designs by Julia Morgan, Bernard Maybeck, and Walter J. Mathews were built to house "friendless" girls. The girls had access to education and medical care. They were taught skills that would enable them to become self-sufficient as adults.

Papai means "daddy" in Portuguese.

Paper clip campaign was a 1998 project started by middle-school students in Whitwell, Tennessee who created a monument for Holocaust victims in Nazi concentration camps. Watch **documentary film, *Paper Clips*.**

Penny arcade was a popular form of amusement in the late nineteenth and early twentieth centuries, typically with miniature novelties inside glass boxes. Visit **Musée Mécanique, Pier 45, San Francisco.**

Peon or *peón* is a term for a day laborer or unskilled farm worker, often used as a pejorative.

Peralta family owned 44,800 acres between El Cerrito and San Leandro, including Oakland. Don Luís Peralta arrived in *Alta California* on the Anza expedition (mid-1770s). In 1820, he received a land grant from the Spanish Crown as a reward for more than three decades of military service. In 1821, the Peraltas built an adobe house on the site of the **Peralta Hacienda Historical Park at 2465 Thirty-Fourth Avenue.** This was the first non-Native American family home in the region. There, Antonio Peralta (Don Luís Peralta's son) came to live with his wife in 1828. His three other brothers soon joined him. In the 1830s and 1840s, the Peralta herds grew to 8,000 head of longhorn cattle and 2,000 horses. By 1842, Don Luís might have been concerned about the encroachment of the Americans and as a precaution, divided his land among his four sons in formal agreements.

In 1846, a small group of U.S. citizens staged an uprising ("Bear Flag Revolt") and declared the California Republic. This revolt helped to launch the U.S.-Mexican War (1846-1848). With the Gold Rush in 1849, the non-Native California population exploded in San Francisco from 1,000 to 25,000.

Although the 1848 U.S.-Mexico treaty honored the land titles of *Californios*, families had to prove the validity of their titles in court. Locally, settlers and speculators squatted on Peralta land, built dwellings, stole and killed Peralta cattle, and even sold parcels of Peralta land as their own. By the time the courts ruled that *Californios* were the legal owners, the land had slipped into others' hands, either paid as legal fees or sold for living expenses. When Antonio Peralta died in 1879, he only owned his Victorian house (built in 1870) and twenty-three acres of land. The Peralta family lived on the premises until 1897.

Peralta Hacienda Historical Park at 2465 Thirty-Fourth Avenue is in the Fruitvale district of Oakland. Visit the house museum, grounds, and special exhibits. Information at **(510) 532-9142** and **www.peraltahacienda.org**. See also *Anza expeditions* and *Californios*.

Pole vendors sold vegetables door-to-door throughout Oakland. Because of anti-Chinese sentiments and laws, they were often harassed, forced to pay an extra tax ("pole tax"), or forbidden to sell goods without a horse and buggy. "Pole tax" is not the same as "poll tax," which requires a payment to vote.

Pullman Palace Car Company (1862-1968) was founded by George Pullman to manufacture railroad cars, including luxury sleepers, which featured elegant furnishings and deluxe customer service. Pullman was once the largest employer of blacks in the United States, working as porters, waiters, cooks, and maids on the cars and providing these deluxe services. See also *Brotherhood of Sleeping Car Porters*.

Queue is a long braid of hair worn down the back, once common for Chinese men.

Rainbow coalition was coined by Fred Hampton (1948-1969) to describe inclusiveness. Hampton was deputy chairman of the Illinois chapter of the Black Panther Party and leader of the Chicago chapter. Watch **documentary films, *The Murder of Fred Hampton*** and an episode in the series, ***Eyes on the Prize***.

Ramada is an open or semi-enclosed shelter, roofed with brush or branches, and designed to provide shade and function as an outdoor living area.

Ranchos were family villages at the center of open range that sustained large herds of cattle, sheep, and horses. Landless Mexicans and Ohlone did most of the work. See also *Peralta family.*

Ration coupons were issued during World War II to restrict consumption of gasoline, sugar, coffee, shoes, butter, meat (except horse meat), and other commodities. A slogan of the era was *Use it up / Wear it out / Make it do / Do without!*

Reata is a lasso or rope used to catch animals.

Reading the world is a term used by Paulo Freire (1921-1997), Brazilian educator and activist. "This movement from the world to the word and from the word to the world is always present, even the spoken word flows from our reading of the world."

Rebozo is a long scarf or shawl covering the head and shoulders, traditionally worn by Latina women.

Redlining refers to the practice of denying, or charging more for, services such as lending, banking, and insurance. In urban areas where people of color lived, red lines on a map indicated where they could not qualify for loans to buy or improve property. The practice contributed to the deterioration and impoverishment of large sections of U.S. cities. The *Fair Housing Act of 1968,* as amended, prohibits redlining based on race, religion, sex, familial status, disability, or ethnic origin. In 1963, California passed the *Rumford Fair Housing Law.* William Byron Rumford was a member of the State Assembly (1948-1966). His 1959 *Fair Employment Practices Act* was also landmark legislation against discrimination.

Red Road is a philosophy inspired by beliefs found in a variety of Native American spiritual teachings about the right path of life.

Restorative healing circles are gatherings in schools, community centers, juvenile halls, and places of worship, where adults and young people can meet to safely express their feelings and help each other heal themselves and their communities.

Restorative justice (RJ) offers a vision and practice for responding to crime and similar injustices by seeking to bring balance, repair, healing, and possibly reconciliation to victims (or surviving family members) and offenders who are willing to engage in restorative work. If the offender is in a California state prison, victims (or surviving family members) may contact the Office of Victim Services of the California Department of Corrections to request assistance in looking into the possibility of a victim-of-fender dialogue. **Office of Victim Services (877) 256-6877** (toll free), **victimservices@cdcr.ca.gov**, and **Office of Victim Services, P.O. Box 942883, Sacramento, CA 94283-0001.**

Restrictive covenant is a device used in real estate contracts to exclude certain ethnic groups from renting, leasing, and buying specific properties. In California, African Americans, Asians, Latinos, and Native Americans have all encountered this form of discrimination. Some argue that this practice of discrimination was positive in one respect because black middle-class families and professionals contributed to the well-being of their old neighborhoods. The practice was ruled illegal in 1948.

Revolutionaries are committed to transforming society and/or government in order to create a new society or government. See also *Black Panther Party* and *Brown Berets.*

Rosie was the symbol of women working in the shipyards and other war industries during World War II. African American women who worked in the shipyards were initially treated like other minorities and given menial jobs. However, many eventually became welders at the Kaiser shipyards. Frances Mary Albrier was a Civil Rights activist and in 1943 became the first black woman to be hired at the Kaiser Shipyard Number Two in Richmond. After the war and as men returned home, many women were laid off or returned to lower-paying, traditional female jobs. Visit **Rosie the Riveter WWII Home Front National Historical Park, 1414 Harbor Way South, Richmond, California**. Information at **(510) 232-5050**. Watch the **documentary film,** *The Life and Times of Rosie the Riveter.* See also *Kaiser shipyards.*

Sampan is a small boat used in China and Japan.

School integration. The Brooklyn Colored School in Oakland at **Tenth Avenue and East Eleventh Street** operated until 1871, when African-American families successfully petitioned the school board to integrate Oakland public schools. Chinese children were not allowed into the California public school system until the 1885 landmark case *Tape v. Hurley* in the California Supreme Court. Afterwards, segregated public schools for Chinese children were established. Ida Louise Jackson (1902-1996), the first African-American teacher in the California public school system, was hired in 1926 to teach in Oakland. *Mendez v. Westminster* was a 1947 ruling that led to the desegregation of all California schools (before *Brown v. Board of Education* desegregated all U.S. public schools in 1954).

Scottish Rite Center, built as a Masonic lodge, is also used for theatrical performances and many other events. It is located at **1547 Lakeside Drive on Lake Merritt.**

Second Gold Rush was used to describe the huge, diverse migration to the Bay Area of men and women seeking jobs in the war industries during World War II.

Sepia-tint and *tintypes* were early photographic processes popular in the nineteenth century.

Seventh Street thrived as a music and entertainment scene with over forty nightclubs and bars. It was the birthplace of West Coast blues, fusing Texas blues and urban swing. In the 1960s, Seventh Street was effectively destroyed by public works projects: I-880 (Cypress freeway), the massive Oakland Main Post Office which demolished twelve blocks, and BART. See also the website of the **Bay Area Blues Society**.

Shellmounds were large heaps of shells and other materials found near Native American settlements. Some also served as gravesites where the community buried their dead. Over 400 shellmounds once ringed San Francisco Bay. Emeryville's shellmound was 60 feet high and 100 yards long. From the 1870s until 1924, Shellmound Pavilion (Emeryville) was an amusement park with a dance hall on top of the shellmound. In 2005, the Bay Street Mall opened on the site of the shellmound. Inside the mall is a commemorative garden. An annual protest against the desecration of an Ohlone sacred site is held at the mall on the Friday after Thanksgiving. It's called "Don't Buy Anything Day." **Historic photographs of local shellmounds before they were destroyed are available online.** See also *Ohlone.*

Sickle cell anemia is a hereditary disease mostly found in Africans or those of African descent. In 1971, the Black Panther Party created an education campaign and screening service at their free health clinics.

Slow violence is a term for chronic social ills that affect the health and well-being of impoverished people, often for generations. (Author's source: talk by activist-scholar, Angela Davis). See also *Violence.*

"Speak Truth to Power" is reputed to be a Quaker phrase dating back to the eighteenth century. It suggests that the power of truth is greater than the power of domination.

Strike is a work stoppage by laborers to protest working conditions, wages, benefits, and/or discrimination, or to support a bargaining position. Oakland has a long labor history that includes many strikes. A "general strike" occurred in Oakland in 1946 to support clerks from two downtown department stores. In support, 100,000 workers from 142 American Federation of Labor (AFL) unions went out on strike. Read **"An Eyewitness Account by Stan Weir: The 1946 Oakland General Strike,"** CounterPunch, November 1, 2011.

Occupy Oakland called for a "general strike" on November 2, 2011. The strike included a mass demonstration in downtown and a march to the Port of Oakland.

Suffrage is the right to vote. Following the Civil War, the Fifteenth Amendment to the U.S. Constitution (1870) prohibited using race, color, or previous servitude as a disqualification for voting. Suffrage was an important women's issue in the nineteenth and early twentieth centuries. *The Carrier Dove* was an Oakland newspaper (1883-1893) devoted to women's suffrage. In California, black women established their own clubs (Oakland Literary Aid Society and State Federation of Colored Women's Clubs). California women won the right to vote in 1911. The Twenty-First Amendment to the U.S. Constitution (1920) recognized women's right to vote nationally.

Tallow is boiled animal fat used to make candles and soap.

Tassa is the nickname for Tassafaronga Village Apartments, a public housing project originally built in 1966 and rebuilt in 2010, located on **Eighty-Fourth Avenue**.

Three-Fifths Compromise (1787) was the enticement that drafters of the Constitution used to persuade southern slaveholding states to join the new union after the American Revolution. For taxation and representation in Congress, enslaved Africans and their offspring would count as three-fifths of a human being.

Temescal is a Nahuatl or Aztec word meaning sweat house.

Tongs are Chinese family associations that provide services to the Chinese community.

Topaz was one of ten internment camps for Japanese and Japanese Americans. Located in central Utah in the Sevier Desert, it reached its maximum population in March 1943 with approximately 8,000 internees. Most internees from Oakland were sent to Topaz. See also *Internment camps*.

Transcontinental railroad was completed on May 10, 1869 when a gold spike was driven into the track at Promontory Summit, Utah. Oakland was the western terminus for the railroad. The first transcontinental train arrived in Oakland on November 8, 1869. Instead of weeks and months, travel across the continent now took approximately eight days.

To build the railroad, many Chinese were employed to tunnel through the mountains. It was slow, dangerous work. By 1911, three transcontinental railroads (Central Pacific, Southern Pacific, and Western Pacific) converged in Oakland. Before the popularity of cars, a total of 1,600 trains (including local streetcars) traveled daily in and around the city. During World War II, Oakland was an important transportation hub for ships, trucks, and trains. See also *Chinese*.

Tule is a large rush that grows in the marshy areas of California.

UFW (United Farm Workers). See also *Farm workers* and *Filipino*.

Union is an organization formed by workers to engage in collective bargaining with employers for better wages, hours, working conditions, benefits, and job security.

Universal Declaration of Human Rights (UDHR) is a declaration adopted by the United Nations General Assembly on December 10, 1948. It represents the first global expression of rights to which all human beings are inherently entitled. Information at **www.un.org.**

Vaqueros (from *vaca* or cow) were herdsmen or cowboys for thousands of head of cattle, horses, and sheep that belonged to *Californios.* They were often Ohlone or landless Mexicans. "Buckaroo" is the English version of *vaquero.*

Vertical gardens are walls with vegetation, common in contemporary green architecture.

Victory gardens were promoted during World War II to decrease food shortages and widen the participation of the war effort.

Violence is a means for a person or group to establish domination over others. Lethal weapons, enslavement, and war are tools of violence. However, chronic poverty, low wages, poor access to health care and quality education are also means of violence. See also *Slow violence.*

Whalers were ships that hunted whales for their oil.

Winnowing basket is shaped to separate grain from chaff.

Workers' compensation is a federal insurance program that protects workers and their families by paying money for injuries and deaths on the job.

YA or *Youth Authority* is the former name of the California Division of Juvenile Justice (DJJ).

Yerba Buena means "good herb." It is the former name of San Francisco. It is the current name of an island in San Francisco Bay.

Yéye is "grandfather" in Chinese.

Zócalo is a public square or plaza in Mexico.

Zoot suit was a style of clothing, especially popular with 1940s Latino subculture.

About
Richmond Tales
Lost Secrets of the Iron Triangle

"*Richmond Tales* is an extraordinary book that artfully uses the power of fiction to provide both an imaginative glimpse into Richmond's past and present, as well as a beautiful vision of what could be in our future. Written for young people, it is a great read for all ages. We are so proud to have this book in our local school district that we made it the Official Book of Richmond!" – Gayle McLaughlin, Mayor, City of Richmond

"Since 2009 *Richmond Tales* has been a favorite of our students not only in schools in Richmond but throughout the West Contra Costa Unified School District. Our students can identify with the neighborhoods and the characters in ways not possible with other books they read. Mario's and Maisha's travel-through-time connects our students to a past they knew little about and future that they hope to be theirs." – Bruce Harter, Superintendent, West Contra Costa Unified School District

"Summer Brenner's *Richmond Tales, Lost Secrets of the Iron Triangle*, has sparked an outbreak of "reading-fever" in the Richmond community because the storyline gives readers a ticket to ride backward and forward in time..." – Tasion Kwamilele, *The Oakland Post*

"The book isn't just for kids, either. Raymond's mom, Adrianne Rosal, said she can't wait to tackle it after her son finishes. West Contra Costa Superintendent Bruce Harter said he can't put the book down. And Barb Johnson, Aide to U.S. Rep. George Miller, D-Martinez, who attended the Thursday book party, had a favor to ask. 'I'm on chapter 29, so don't anyone tell me the end of it yet.'" – Kimberly Wetzel, *Contra Costa Times*

"I don't want to spoil the ending for you, suffice it to say that an incredibly exciting reveal awaits our courageous young people, who learn that once you get the big picture, your lives can never seem small again." – Kevin Killian, poet, playwright, and author of *Tweaky Village*

Summer Brenner is the author of a dozen works of poetry and fiction, including novels for youth. *Ivy, Homeless in San Francisco* was the winner of the Children's Literary Classics and Moonbeam Children's Book awards. *Richmond Tales, Lost Secrets of the Iron Triangle* received a Richmond Historic Preservation award and was produced as a play by the East Bay Center for Performing Arts with Richmond Rotary. Her writings have appeared in dozens of anthologies and literary magazines. She has given scores of readings in the United States, France, and Japan. *The Los Angeles Times:* "She is the author as choreographer, a moving force with a pen." *The Economist:* "You should be reading Summer Brenner." In 2013, she received an award from the City of Richmond's Human Rights and Human Relations Commission.

Miguel Bounce Perez is a muralist and designer with an additional focus on photography and video. Originally raised in Berkeley, California, his "home base" currently shifts between Oakland and Mexico. In 2007, he appropriated his father's low-rider car club and opened a community art space and showroom in Berkeley under the same name, Pueblo Nuevo. In addition to curating exhibits, Miguel keeps the Pueblo Nuevo name and mission alive by creating space for collaborative productions and artistic exchanges everywhere he goes. He mostly travels with friends and family, otherwise known as Trust Your Struggle. Trust Your Struggle is a collective of visual artists, educators, and activists dedicated to social justice and community building through the medium of art. Miguel's artwork and murals have been featured publicly and in galleries across the United States from New York to California as well as the Philippines, Puerto Rico, Cuba, Dominican Republic, Guatemala, Nicaragua, Colombia, Mexico, and the United Kingdom.